"This has gone far enough!"
Sabina decided

"You'd better go and tell everyone that we're not engaged after all," she told Yorke loftily.

Flint glinted in his eyes as he silently studied her. "I will—when you've given me back that ring."

Again it was impasse. Since she wasn't getting anywhere by firing up to him, might she not have the satisfaction of making him squirm? So she smiled. He held her glance.

"Do you know, Yorke, I do believe I shall quite enjoy being engaged to you."

Then, with not a squirm in sight, Yorke leaned back fractionally—and grinned.

Dear Reader,

The fortieth anniversary of Harlequin Romance this year coincides with the pearl anniversary of the Steele romance. Peter and I have been married for thirty years in September.

I have always had a lot of ideas for writing romance fiction, but without Peter's enormous encouragement, I would never have started to write a romance novel.

I have no notion where the ideas for my stories come from. All I know is that I sit down at my desk and sort through one theme after another until I find a story that I feel I would really like to write and that you, my reader, would really like to read.

I do so hope you enjoy reading *With His Ring*. I'll let you into a little secret—this book is one of my favorites.

Very sincerely,

Jessica Steele.

With His Ring
Jessica Steele

Harlequin Books

TORONTO • NEW YORK • LONDON
AMSTERDAM • PARIS • SYDNEY • HAMBURG
STOCKHOLM • ATHENS • TOKYO • MILAN
MADRID • WARSAW • BUDAPEST • AUCKLAND

ISBN 0-373-03459-8

WITH HIS RING

First North American Publication 1997.

Copyright © 1996 by Jessica Steele.

CHAPTER ONE

SABINA took a cup of coffee over to a chair in the sitting room and sat down to reflect that it was quiet in the apartment without Natalie. Not that Natalie was noisy, it was just that now that her friend had gone—it was quiet without her.

They had been friends from schooldays, she and Natalie, but it had only been three months ago that Sabina had moved in with her. Well, not moved in with her exactly, for she had known in advance that Natalie would soon be setting off on her semi-backpacking-around-the-world adventure, and she would then have the apartment to herself.

'Come with me, Sabbie,' Natalie had urged.

It was an exciting thought, but Sabina had rejected it. 'I don't think my parents...' she'd begun, and had had no need to say any more.

'I forgot. Your parents,' Natalie had apologised, having spent more time with Sabina's parents than with her own.

That conversation had taken place almost four months ago, Sabina reflected, and went on to consider how her parents had been in their forties when she, an only and much wanted baby, had been born. Her parents loved her to pieces, she knew that, just as she loved them. Which was probably why she was frequently assailed by feelings of guilt when she found their love, their need to keep her safe, just a touch too over-protective.

They tried not to be over-protective; she was aware of that in the way they encouraged her to bring her friends home. Not that she had too many friends because, perhaps because of her sheltered upbringing, she had grown up a cautious child.

Which was why, she mused, it was a little amazing that, being so cautious, tentative maybe, about making friends, she and adventurous, tackle-anything Natalie had, out of all the other girls at their school, become best friends.

To start with, her parents had not liked Natalie, with her sharp, couldn't-care-less front. But as they'd gradually got to know her and had become more aware of the many times she had been let down by either one of her parents or the other—sometimes both—they'd begun to feel sorry for her and started to warm to her.

She and Natalie had left school and gone to business college together, and while Sabina had gone to work for her father Natalie, an attractive blonde, had taken one secretarial job after another. Natalie's first job had come to grief when she'd fallen in love with her boss, thought he was in love with her—for he had said so—only to find her idol had feet of clay when he'd gone and married someone else. People were always letting Natalie down.

'It's the last time!' Natalie had declared, and had gone on to her second and then third love affair, both of which had gone disastrously wrong. And Sabina had feared for her. Natalie, who'd had so little love in her life, was looking for love, and was still being let down by those she loved.

Natalie had been truly off men when she'd told Sabina that she'd had enough of men and her present job and that she was going to go around the world. Money was not too much of a problem—she had a small allowance from her father, given, she said, in place of affection.

Sabina, at twenty-two, felt she should have been able to make up her own mind about going abroad with her friend, but was unsure if it was the fact that 'backpacking' was not truly her or if it was respect for her parents that had caused her not to want to make an issue of it. She'd known in advance that her parents would find a hundred and one very sound reasons why she should not go off—two young women abroad alone—for the best part of a year.

However, when, on her meeting with her friend, Natalie had put forward another suggestion—that she come and 'house-sit' her flat while she was away—Sabina had not been able to deny that the idea had tremendous appeal.

'As you know I subleased the apartment from Oliver when he decided to buy something. But I'd hate it if he found another subtenant while I'm gone.' Oliver Robbins was a lovable and harmless friend who came from the same Surrey village as Sabina. She had introduced him to Natalie ages ago, and now all three were excellent friends. Oliver had left Wolverdene to move closer to London some time since. But, while Sabina was certain he would not dream of re-subletting the apartment, it just proved once again how, used to being let down by people, Natalie was having trouble trusting even their very close friend. 'Say no if you think it will cause too much of a rumpus with your parents,' Natalie had gone on, 'but you were saying not so long ago how you wouldn't mind your own place.'

'That's true,' Sabina had agreed, and had felt greatly touched that in asking her to take over her apartment for a while Natalie was in effect saying that she trusted her, and felt that she would never let her down. 'And I'd love to move in, I really would.' She'd paused, and then, realising that this was something she wanted more than anything, said, 'I'll chat it over with my parents tonight and let you know tomorrow.'

'I've a spare bedroom if you want to move in straight away,' Natalie had suggested—and it had been left at that.

When Sabina had next seen her friend she had been in lengthy discussions with her parents. They had raised many objections but, doing their very best to be fair, they had at last consented to her leaving her very comfortable home. 'London isn't so very far away,' her mother had smiled bravely.

'Oh, Mum!' Sabina had cried, and had gone over and given her a hug.

She had moved in with Natalie two weeks later, and in the month that followed, while her mother initially rang most every evening, Sabina discovered that her father had been right in his assertion that she would not find it as easy to travel to work as she had.

There were several more conveniently placed secretarial jobs advertised in the paper—but how to tell him that she wanted to leave the firm he had started so many years ago?

There was only one way—honestly. 'Would you mind very much if I found a job nearer to Natalie's flat?' she had gathered her courage to ask.

'You're saying you want to leave your daddy?' he teased.

'Oh, Dad,' she groaned.

'All right, poppet, let's be serious,' he said, and paid her the wonderful compliment of treating her as a grownup and not his little girl by telling her how he had been thinking for some while of selling his component manufacturing business. 'I'm sixty-five next year, as you know. And while you've more than pulled your weight I'm fully aware that you aren't interested in taking the business over.'

'If only I'd been born a boy,' she smiled.

'You'd have saved me a lot of worry,' her father sighed, and grinned and went on to tell her of his thoughts for finding someone who might want to take over a going concern. 'Either that or get a manager in,' he ended. 'But, getting back to your problem—you'll be a gem for anyone who takes you on.'

'You're biased,' she laughed, and loved him lots, for he had in effect just given her his blessing to work elsewhere.

On a Monday six weeks later Sabina had started to work at Alpha Computers, a firm situated but a twenty-minute drive from where she and Natalie lived. She came back to the apartment that first evening to tell Natalie all about it, and to repeat everything to her mother when she rang to ask how her day had gone.

The next day she got more into her secretarial role and met a man from another department whom she rather took to. Chris Dawson was about four years older than herself, and looked at her in a friendly fashion. 'You're a vast improvement on Adrian Wallace's previous secretary,' he declared, openly admiring her shoulder-length night-black hair and her creamy skin.

Like him or not, she had an inbuilt caution, and, 'Thank you,' she murmured, and returned swiftly to her office.

She went home that evening thinking about Chris Dawson and entered the apartment musing that she might mention him to Natalie. But the never-before-seen dreamy look on Natalie's face when she went in told her that something pretty momentous had happened to her friend that day.

'Are you going to tell me about it?' Sabina asked her, noticing how her non-sugar-taking friend was spooning sugar into her tea.

'Is it so noticeable?' Natalie questioned, looking a touch panicky.

'What happened?'

'I met the most divine man today,' Natalie breathed. 'Oh, Sabbie,' she cried, 'I'm in love—and this time it's for real!'

Sabina's heart sank. Even as she prayed that this time Natalie would not be let down, her anxieties grew. Natalie had been checking out some lightweight yet sturdy luggage, it appeared, when out of the blue another customer had come over and had started to give his opinion on the merits or otherwise of the luggage she was thinking of buying for her trip.

'One thing led to another,' Natalie revealed, 'and the next thing I know is that I'm having a cup of coffee with him in the café next door, and, following on from that, I'm having dinner with him tonight.'

'Oh, Natalie!' Sabina exclaimed, she the one panicking now. 'You don't know the first thing about him!'

'Did I ever mention that you're just a hint on the too careful side?' Natalie smiled.

Over the two weeks that followed it seemed that Natalie saw Rod Lacey at almost every waking moment. And, from Sabina's observation when he brought Natalie home each night, he seemed to be as much taken with Natalie as she was with him.

But still Sabina feared for her friend. She had been let down so often in the past. Natalie had said nothing of changing her plan to travel the globe—would the feelings this man had for Natalie be strong enough to survive the long months of parting?

Such anxieties occupied much of Sabina's thoughts right up until the Sunday prior to her friend's departure the following day. But as soon as Natalie and Rod came in that Sunday evening she knew from the expression on both their faces that something quite tremendous had happened.

'Look!' Natalie cried, and opened her palm to show her the most exquisite antique-set emerald and diamond engagement ring.

Sabina was both flabbergasted and overjoyed all at the same time, and amid congratulations and good wishes she learned, with more joy, that while Natalie still wanted to go on her travels Rod was adamant that she would not go alone. He, with Natalie not raising the smallest objection, was going with her.

Rod Lacey went up a great deal in Sabina's estimation. He was a tallish man of about twenty-eight, and fairly good-looking, she supposed, though she thought that his mouth was just a whisper on the weak side. But that he was prepared to throw up his career to go with Natalie—not that anyone had said what work he did— just seemed to prove how very much he loved her friend.

'Come and talk to me while I check my luggage to see what, if anything, I can leave behind,' Natalie suggested when she came back from saying goodnight to her fiancé.

In actual fact, however, it was mainly Natalie who did the talking as she exclaimed again and again, with wonder, that as she had fallen in love with Rod at first sight, so too had he fallen in love at first sight with her.

'When did he ask you to marry him?' Sabina, feeling a touch dreamy herself, could not resist asking.

'This afternoon,' Natalie replied, and drifted off for a moment or two before going on to reveal, 'He bought the ring yesterday. Sold his car to pay for it.'

'Greater love hath no man!' Sabina exclaimed, impressed. Natalie threw a pillow at her.

'But you're right, of course,' she agreed, holding the ring out again so they could both admire it. 'He's saved some of the money for our trip, but this ring must have cost thousands!'

'It must have,' Sabina concurred.

'Which is part of the reason why, unfortunately, I'll have to leave it behind.'

'You're not taking it with you? You're not going to wear it?'

'That's the other reason. Darling, wonderful man that he is, he hasn't been very observant about my stubby, not to say podgy fingers. It doesn't fit!' she added succinctly. 'And since there isn't time for us to have it made bigger before we go—not to mention that, while I hope there'll be few times when we'll be really roughing it, I don't want to run the risk of it being stolen should we find ourselves camping out in a not too salubrious part of the world.'

'You've had all your jabs?' Sabina asked urgently.

'I have. But thanks for asking, Sabbie—my mother didn't bother.'

All that had taken place a week ago—and yes, Sabina decided, it was most definitely quiet without Natalie there. Wondering when Natalie might think to drop her a card, Sabina picked up her used coffee-cup and saucer and took them out to the kitchen. She was in the act of rinsing them, however, when the intercom system sounded to alert her that someone had pressed the outside bell.

Sabina went out into the hall. She was not expecting anyone to call, though it was not unknown for Oliver Robbins to drop by for a chat or to ask them out for a drink or even dinner.

She picked up the intercom phone. 'Hello?' she queried.

'Natalie Harris?' queried a voice in return.

It was a voice Sabina did not recognise. Deep, cultured, masculine—authoritative. It was on the tip of her tongue to explain that Natalie had gone away. Then her inbuilt caution sprang to the fore. The name above the doorbell said Natalie Harris—her own name had never been added. And, despite the cultured tones, it could be just about anybody out there.

'Well?' queried the voice sharply—clearly not the most patient of men.

'Who wants her?' Sabina, not liking his tone one little bit, returned just as sharply.

An impatient grunt was her initial answer. Followed by the short reply of, 'Yorke Mackinnon.' And, while the name seemed familiar, as if she had heard it before somewhere, he added, 'I'm Rodney Lacey's cousin—I need to get in touch with him.'

Sabina relaxed a trifle. This was no speculative caller bent on some opportunistic crime, but a relative of Rod's. And plainly, even though she could not recall any conversation with Rod where he had mentioned his cousin by name, Rod must have done for the name Yorke Mackinnon to sound as familiar as it did.

It was early June, the weather pleasant, but, while she had no more idea than the general direction in which Natalie and Rod were travelling, it seemed churlish, not to say downright rude to carry on a conversation with his cousin through a speaker at the front door.

She pressed the door-release mechanism and, for some unknown reason, scooted to her bedroom to check her appearance. Serious wide brown eyes stared back at her. She flicked her glance over her long-legged, slender shape, jeans and T-shirt-clad, and hastily ran a comb through her hair. Then she threw the comb down in disgust. Good grief, all this because some bossy-sounding cousin of Rod Lacey had called needing to get in touch with him? A bossy cousin she didn't even know!

The apartment doorbell sounded and a few seconds later she was looking at this man she did not know. She was fairly tall herself, but had to look a long way up, for he was taller than average—and had been way at the front when good looks had been handed out. He was somewhere in his mid-thirties, dark-haired and, as she stared, she observed that he had the most sensational dark blue eyes.

'Miss Harris?' he enquired coolly, having observed her in return in one all-assessing glance but clearly in no way similarly taken out of his stride by her looks, which, she recalled—and somehow needed at that moment to recall—had once been termed little short of sensational too.

'C-come in,' she stammered, realising belatedly that what she should have been telling him was that she was not Miss Harris.

Sabina led the way into the average-sized, averagely furnished sitting room, and turned to rectify her omission when Yorke Mackinnon promptly took the initiative from her by demanding, 'Where is he?'

Sabina looked at him, startled. He might well be immaculately suited and every bit the city gent, but she cared for his manner not one little bit. 'Rod...?'

'Who else?' he grunted—and she sorely wished she had left him standing on the doorstep.

'He's not here!'

'I can see that!' he returned testily. 'Have you seen him this evening?'

'You don't know!' she gasped. Quite plainly, cousin though he might be, this man had no idea that his relative had taken a hydrofoil to France six days ago and was likely to be out of the country for some quite considerable time.

Yorke Mackinnon stilled, stared at her, and, all too obviously not a man slow on the uptake, said, 'You'd better tell me.'

Just like that—bossy brute! Should she, shouldn't she? She had no intention whatsoever of breaking any of Natalie's confidences, nor Rod's either, although up until this moment she had not considered the fact that the two of them were exploring the globe was in any way confidential.

'There's nothing to tell,' she replied stubbornly—and could see from the acid glint that came to those dark eyes that she had not endeared herself to this man any.

She had no idea why he was looking for Rod, but she did not care for the way Rod's cousin studied her for some silent seconds, almost as if—coming to terms with the fact that if he was to get any information from her he must first reveal some of why he wanted to see Rod— he was deciding just how little he could get away with telling her.

Sabina started to bridle—she had not felt too well disposed to this man before. And she was left slightly floundering when, taking a casual look about him, giving her the impression that there was no urgency about his visit, he enquired coolly, 'You've seen the ring, of course?'

Her mouth fell slightly open. For him to know about the lovely antique emerald and diamond engagement ring which Rod had given to Natalie must mean that he had seen him in between the time Rod had purchased it last Saturday and had given it to Natalie on Sunday.

'I have, and it's beautiful,' she could see no harm in confirming.

'But he no longer has it?' Yorke Mackinnon was in as quick as a flash.

Feeling slightly winded—never had she met such a man—Sabina opened her mouth, and closed it again. Although, on thinking about it, since Rod had given the ring to Natalie on their engagement, in reality the ring was no longer in his possession.

'Well, no. But what—?'

'He's sold it?' Yorke Mackinnon cut in aggressively.

Sabina stared at him in astonishment, her annoyance at being interrupted before she could ask what the dickens he thought it had to do with him, vanishing at his tone, at what he said.

'Sold it!' she echoed. 'Why would he sell it? He only bought it last Saturday!' With no small satisfaction she saw that her last remark had stopped the man in his tracks.

Her small feeling of satisfaction was short-lived. For it did not take him very long to recover, and, 'Did he now?' he questioned sharply. 'He told you that?'

'Well, no,' she answered—in all honesty, it had been Natalie who had told her. 'But Na—'

Yorke Mackinnon cut her off again—she was getting a bit tired of him—to change tack and demand, 'So why then would he buy such an item?'

'You don't think the reason's obvious?' Sabina snapped—and was again astonished when he did no more than stride forward and with a grip that made her skin tingle, take a hold of her left hand and raise it to inspect her totally ringless fingers.

'You're engaged?' he snarled, clearly neither liking nor believing in the notion.

She had had enough. 'Not me!' she flared, snatching her hand back. 'Natalie!'

'Natalie!' And, as quick as ever—and just as disagreeable—'If you're not Natalie Harris, who the hell are you?' he charged.

Sabina felt a fool, and didn't like it. She should, she knew, have told him straight away that she was not Natalie. 'If you'd given me half a chance I'd have told you,' she accused, determined not to be made to feel an idiot. 'My name's Sabina Constable and I share this apartment with Natalie. Well, that is...' Her innate honesty tripped her up, that and a sort of confusion this dreadful man evoked in her, and she found she was rushing to explain, 'Well, I did share with Natalie for a few months, but now I'm—er—sort of more—er—care-taking the apartment while she's away.'

'She's away?' he took up at once, and, sharper than a tack, 'Where have they gone?' he barked.

Really! This man! Who *did* he think he was? 'Round the world!' she fired hotly. 'And, in answer to your next question, I don't know when they'll be back—they could be away a whole year!' With sparks of fury flashing in her eyes—never had she felt so angry—Sabina glared at him. She saw his glance on her pause, stray to what she guessed were splashes of outraged colour in her otherwise creamy cheeks, but she did not care. Heartily did she wish she had never let him in. The ignorant, ill-mannered brute, to come barking his arrogant way in. 'I'll show you out!' she hissed as she reached a full head of steam.

He moved not a fraction, but stayed to demand, 'They've taken it with them?'

'What?' She felt left-footed again.

'The ring!' he replied irritatedly, for all the world as if he viewed her as the idiot he had made her feel. 'They've taken the ring with them?'

Why Natalie's engagement ring was of such importance to him was a mystery to her. But just then Sabina was more interested in making him the one to feel a fool for a change rather than in delving into mysteries that did not exactly concern her.

'Of course not!' She helped him to a generous portion of her own arrogance. 'Since they intend to keep well away from anywhere touristy, they might find themselves well in some lawless back of beyond. Besides which,' she added for lofty good measure, 'Rob didn't get the ring size quite right, so it will have to be altered before Natalie can wear it.'

Yorke Mackinnon studied her for about one second. 'So it's here, in this apartment?'

She could see no good reason to deny it. 'Got it in one,' she confirmed—and discovered that he was as quick with his orders as with everything else.

'You'd better let me have it,' he stated, every bit as if he thought that that was all there was to it!

At that moment Sabina would have liked nothing better than to let him have it—right between the eyes. But, with regard to Natalie's beautiful ring, she'd see him in hell first. 'Now, if you don't mind,' she suggested sweetly, 'I really will show you out.'

She had taken a few steps in the direction of the door, when his voice stopped her. 'I am not,' he clipped categorically, 'going anywhere without that ring.'

He, Sabina at that moment decided, was not the only one who could get tough. And, it being the case that he was too big for her to attempt to throw out, she walked back to him and eyed the good-looking odious whole of him. Then, sliding her glance from his expensively clad feet up the long, long, lean but broad-shouldered length of him, she deliberately switched her gaze from him to the shortness of Natalie's two-seater couch. Then, pleasantly, she turned her gaze back to him, and, as any nicely brought up young woman would, she politely warned him, 'As you wish, Mr Mackinnon, but I'm awfully afraid you're going to ache more than somewhat come morning.'

He stared at her, and she stared at him, and, had she not been well on the way to believing that none of this was happening, she could well have believed that she saw a minuscule twitch of amusement try to have its way at the corners of his most personable mouth.

The smile did not make it. And, to show just how wrong she had got it to think for even an infinitesimal moment that she might have amused him, there was nothing but hostility in both his look and his tone when he grated, 'That ring doesn't belong to you!'

'It doesn't belong to you either!' she retaliated—and was all but floored by his reply.

'It's been in my family since my great-great-grandfather gave it to my great-great-grandmother,' he retorted.

And a sick feeling hit Sabina full square in the stomach. Rod had told Natalie he had bought the ring! Oh, no, not another of Natalie's idols to have feet of clay!

'I don't believe you!' she managed stoutly—and saw when his eyes narrowed that he did not care too well that she had as good as called him a liar.

'Should I need to, I can prove that ring belongs in my family,' he stated sharply, and sounded so positive that again a sick feeling smote Sabina.

But she rallied. People were always letting Natalie down; she, she vowed, would not. 'The ring will still be in your family when Natalie and Rob return and get married,' she told him firmly.

'Then I'm sure you'll have no objection if I keep it until their return,' he changed tack to answer smoothly, never at a loss, it seemed.

'No way,' she refused, shaking her head, rushing on when it looked as if he might have something short and sharp to say about her refusal. 'Apart from anything else, I'm not in the habit of going into Natalie's room and rummaging around in her belongings.'

'I'll do it!' he promptly volunteered—so promptly that *she* almost smiled.

But she refused to be amused. 'No, you won't!' she told him bluntly.

He gave her a look which told her he thought her tedious. 'You're sure it's here?' he grunted. She knew it was—Natalie had shown her its hiding place—and she was somehow reminded that he had initially considered Rob might have sold the ring.

'I'll take a look for it,' she relented sufficiently to offer, adding quickly, cautiously, 'When you've gone.'

'When I've gone?'

It did sound quaint, she had to admit. He, by the sound of it, had called with one purpose only in mind—to see and take that emerald and diamond ring with him. Well, tough—and, since he was such a brute, Sabina could not see any good reason why she should stop being blunt.

'You'll forgive me,' she smiled, 'but you could be anyone for all I know. And,' she tacked on frankly, 'that ring belongs to Natalie—not you.'

She weathered the icy look that showed he had no time for her phoney smiles, nor little time for her either, then, his bluntness knocking hers flying, he gritted, 'That ring does *not* belong to Natalie Harris as you claim, Miss Constable, but happens to be a ring which Rodney Lacey *stole* from me.'

'He st...' She could not go on. Rod had *stolen* the ring he had given to Natalie! Oh, no! He couldn't have. Could he? Oh, poor, poor Natalie. Sabina's spirits hit rock-bottom on her friend's behalf. But she struggled out of the mass of emotional thoughts that were sinking her—she wouldn't believe it; she couldn't believe it. There must be some explanation. 'You're saying that it's your ring?' she questioned, and then, for no good reason that she could think of other than that she was having trouble making sense of any of it just then, asked, 'You were going to get engaged yourself? Er—perhaps give it to your wife?'

'I'm neither married nor thinking of giving up my freedom!' he informed her arrogantly. 'I was holding the ring for my grandmother!' And all of a sudden, seeming to become too impatient with her and the whole sorry business to want to spend any more of his valuable time in trying to get past her stubbornness to go and find what he plainly saw as his property, he took a couple of cards from his wallet, scribbled on one of them. And, obviously having taken on board her ' ... you could be anyone for all I know', he thrust the cards into her hands, gritted, 'Check me out,' and, without a please, thank you or goodnight, he turned and strode from the apartment.

Sabina stared dumbstruck after him, and all of five seconds had passed after him angrily pulling the door to behind him before she thought to glance down at the cards in her hand.

'Oh, grief!' she croaked aloud as first she took in Yorke Mackinnon's address on his personal card, which she recognised as a millionaire's row kind of address in London, and—'Oh my lord!' she gasped as she read his business card, to which he'd added the telephone number of his private line at his office. No wonder she'd thought his name was familiar! He was head of Mackinnon Telecommunication Equipment Manufacturers, that was all! A forward-looking company that was forever in the papers.

Sabina sank down onto the couch. She had felt all trembly inside before. But, oh, help, he was *that* Mackinnon!

Five minutes had passed before she had got herself more of one piece. By then she was not certain which had shaken her more, her encounter with the man—for her life to date had pottered on in a gentle way, with nothing too out of the way to ripple the water—or the fact of learning who he was.

But, more shaking yet, she suddenly realised, was the fact that, from Yorke Mackinnon's invitation to check him out, he had also been telling her that—having given her time to do that—he would be back.

Oh, heavens, just *one* visit from him was one too many!

CHAPTER TWO

THE night was long. Sabina slept only fitfully, and was frequently awake with one thought dominating her mind. People were always letting Natalie down—but she never would. When she slept, she dreamt of a man with dark blue eyes.

Sabina was glad to see daylight and left her bed on Monday feeling exceedingly cross with one Yorke Mackinnon for arriving unheralded and unwanted into her life to give her problems she did not need.

She was not feeling too well disposed to his cousin either, and again began to fear for her friend. Had Rod stolen that ring, and not purchased it as he had told Natalie? Oh, heavens, Natalie had declared that she was truly in love this time! Was she really tangled up with someone who was a thief?

Sabina did not want to believe it, and she began to hate Yorke Mackinnon that he should have come along and spoiled everything. Though when honesty could not be avoided she owned that he could hardly be blamed if his cousin had sticky fingers and had stolen the ring from him.

And that was another mystery. He had said, albeit with scant patience, that the ring was not his either, but that he was holding it for his grandmother. So why was he holding it? And, since Rod was his cousin, his grandmother must be Rod Lacey's grandmother too. So why should Rod not hold what in Sabina's thoughts was now becoming that 'wretched' ring equally well?

Sabina shied away from what would be a painful truth—that his grandmother knew Rod well enough to know that he might not keep the ring secure for her. Instead Sabina wondered why their grandmother would need anyone to hold it for her in the first place. Perhaps she had recently been burgled. Perhaps...

Her thoughts drifted away from what was pure speculation, and she concentrated on fact. The major fact being that Yorke Mackinnon wanted that ring and she was not going to let him have it. She had the ring. She had found it last night in the toe of one of Natalie's winter boots—a place where she kept anything of value. But *he* was not having it, no way! Natalie had been overjoyed with the ring. It said somebody loved her.

Sabina left the apartment and went out to her car, which, because the garage housed Natalie's car, was parked on the standing area in front of it. She went off to work knowing, indelibly, that she just could not hand that ring over to anyone.

That settled upon, she arrived at her office of the opinion that she could now concentrate her thoughts on the job she was being paid to do—and an hour later, her thoughts having drifted time and time again to a good-looking man with dark blue eyes, Sabina pushed her work away from her. She reached into her handbag for the two pieces of card she had last evening placed in there.

Any hope, however, that the man calling himself Yorke Mackinnon might be some bogus con man in possession of his business and private cards was doomed when, acting on impulse, she reached for the phone.

'Mackinnon Telecommunication Equipment,' was the answer she received from the number she had dialled— and, recalling Yorke Mackinnon's 'Check me out', knew that at least that phone number was correct.

By withholding her name but insisting that her call was personal, Sabina managed to get through to his office. It was as far as she got. A pleasant-sounding, unflappable and serene PA blocked her call and Sabina realised that unless she was ready to divulge a little more information Mr Mackinnon was going to remain 'unavailable at the moment'.

'Not to worry,' she told the PA cheerfully. 'I'll ring later.'

Sabina put the phone down and, having established that his business card was authentic, she studied the private line number he had jotted down. She reached for the phone a second time. He had said, 'Check me out,' hadn't he? Had it been guaranteed that she would not hear from him again, she would not have bothered. But, since her every intelligence told her that he was a man who once on the trail—in this case the trail of that ring— would never give up, check him out she would.

She dialled again, and the same pleasant, unflappable, serene voice answered, this time with a name. 'Louise Page,' she stated pleasantly.

Sabina took a deep breath and, hoping Louise Page would not in turn recognise her voice, enquired, 'Er— is Yorke there?'

Miracles! 'Just a moment,' the PA replied—and a second or two later another voice came down the line, a deep, cultured, all-masculine voice.

A voice she would know anywhere, for all he said was an enquiring, 'Hello?'

She swallowed, felt all peculiar inside suddenly—and fought valiantly to overcome it. 'Who is that?' she asked needlessly, just the same.

There was a slight pause before he answered. 'Yorke Mackinnon,' he replied, adding, 'Though since you've called this number you already know that, don't you—Sabina?'

'Just checking,' she commented, and quickly rang off. She was trembling! It was ridiculous! Either he gave his private business number to very few or, as she had recognised his voice, he too had recognised hers—so why was she trembling?

By lunchtime she felt she had herself under control. She had managed to catch up on work she had only toyed with during her first hour, and left her desk with a small feeling of satisfaction about that—and bumped into Chris Dawson on her way out of the building.

Though not exactly 'bumped', it appeared. For, 'I've been looking for you—you weren't in your office,' he said, falling into step with her.

'What can I do for you?' she offered. She didn't normally do his typing, but if he wanted something typed she dared say she could fit it in.

'You could come out with me tonight!' he answered in a rush—and Sabina was caught completely off guard and didn't know how to answer.

Which in no way explained why she should suddenly have a picture of Yorke Mackinnon in her mind's eye. It confused her. 'I'm sorry—I can't tonight,' she told him jerkily, and went on her way to lunch wondering what on earth was the matter with her.

It was true she had only known Chris Dawson two weeks, but he seemed harmless enough. And, up until today, she would have thought she would quite like to go out with him. So why had she said no? And why, for goodness' sake, had Yorke Mackinnon come into her head when she'd been considering her answer?

Confound the man! It was that wretched ring, of course—or rather, the worry over it.

Sabina went home still worrying about the ring and the unhappy likelihood that Natalie had, yet again, fallen for someone unworthy of her, then, at around a quarter to seven that evening, the telephone rang.

Her mother, was her first guess. Then it occurred to her, causing her to hesitate to pick up the phone, that maybe Natalie had thought to give her a quick call to say how everything was going. Oh, heavens, how did one go about suggesting that the man Natalie loved might have stolen the engagement ring he had given her? Knowing that her tact was going to be stretched to its limits, Sabina picked up the receiver—and very nearly dropped it.

'I've been waiting for you to contact me!' snarled a cultured, arrogant pig of a man's voice.

'I did!' she slammed back. 'How did you get this number?'

'It's on the dial!' he grunted—observant, number automatically filed and remembered, not in it. 'Have you found it?' He wasted no more of his valuable time.

It had never been lost, but it was at that point that Sabina wished that she had been born a liar. She opened her mouth to tell him no. 'Yes,' she replied shortly.

'Good! I'll come and collect it!' he retorted before she could draw another breath.

'Save yourself a journey!' she snapped.

'Meaning?'

He wasn't that thick! In point of fact he was the sharpest man she had ever come across. 'I'm not going to let you have it,' she changed tack to enlighten him pleasantly.

He was not impressed. 'You're refusing to hand it over?' he barked.

'It isn't mine to hand over to anyone,' she explained—reasonably, she thought. And had her ears singed for her trouble.

'It isn't yours to keep!' he roared.

There was no answer to that. Quietly, Sabina put down her phone.

She spent the next ten minutes cross and on edge, fully expecting Yorke Mackinnon to ring her again. Without question he would not care for anyone putting the phone down on him.

Not that she was bothered whether he cared or not. But, if he was minded to press the redial button in order to give her ears a blasting, he could go whistle. She was fully resolved that if her phone did ring again she would not answer it.

When that ten minutes stretched to twenty minutes and still her phone stayed quiet, Sabina began to relax.

It was a mistake. A mistake to relax. She knew that when, that twenty minutes having stretched to half an hour and the phone still having stayed quiet, there was a sound to be heard penetrating the silence of the apartment. It was not the sound of a telephone ringing but the buzzing sound of someone ringing the outer doorbell.

Oliver, she prayed, but even as she went to find out she knew in her heart of hearts who it was. 'Hello?' she enquired down the door telephone.

'Mackinnon!' he clipped.

'What do you want?'

He did not deign to answer. Damn him, damn him to hell. Viciously she stabbed at the button to enable him to let himself in—and wished she were poking her finger in his eye.

My heavens! When had she ever grown so pugnacious? Feeling staggered at the way her thoughts had gone, Sabina could only blame him. And then he was but yards away, ringing her doorbell.

She swallowed hard, seemed to need a second or two to gain some control before she went to open the apartment door.

He was as tall and every bit as good-looking as he had been yesterday, she saw, but even now having let him into the building, she was not prepared to invite him into the apartment.

'Well?' she enquired crisply.

He stared down at her, those dark eyes glinting. Sabina refused to swallow again—she wasn't afraid of him!

'In answer to your question—you know what I want!' he stated grimly.

'And you,' she countered, 'know the answer to that!'

The glint in his eyes hardened, but she wasn't budging. His chin jutted—and so did hers. Angrily she glared at him and, quietly seething, he stared at her. Then all at once, even while they exchanged hostile looks, he seemed to think a change of tactics was called for.

That was all Sabina could put it down to anyway. Because one moment they were squaring up to each other, and he was looking at her as if about to give her a verbal battering—let him try!—and then he seemed to pause. To pause as though seeing something in the stubborn set of her chin that suggested he was on a hiding to nothing there.

And suddenly his harsh expression was relenting and there was almost a coaxing note in his voice when he suggested mildly, 'We're getting nowhere by being angry, Sabina. Let's discuss it.'

My stars! Just his change of tone was shattering! She hoped she was never on the other end if he chose to assault her with his charm. Don't be ridiculous! Abruptly Sabina pulled herself together. 'There's nothing to discuss!' she responded tartly—and glared at him.

He smiled, and she tried her best to keep hostile. But that smile, that lightening of his expression was something else again—as was he when he dropped his aggressive manner. And she was weakening; she knew that she was. And that was before, with a charm every bit as devastating as she had thought, he went on to state, 'I've missed my dinner to come to see you.' Sabina eyed him coldly, waiting for him to go—and was absolutely astounded when he went on to charm, and to smile, and to further suggest, 'I don't suppose you'd like to make me a sandwich?'

What she would have liked to do was to tell him to go to hell—so why did she find herself telling him, 'I've only got tinned salmon.'?

'My favourite,' he assured her before she could get herself of one piece to add, And you're having none of it.

Perhaps it was because she felt in need of some space to do just that—get herself more of one piece—that she left him and went into the kitchen to get out the makings for his sandwich.

Once she was in the kitchen, though, and aware that Yorke Mackinnon had followed her inside the apartment, she began to feel anxious that he might start nosing around searching for Natalie's jewel box. Not that the ring was in there. But Sabina had turned and was about to hastily go and see what he was up to, when Yorke Mackinnon strolled into the kitchen.

'I'll put the kettle on for that coffee you're going to make me,' he remarked easily—and Sabina went through a welter of conflicting emotions.

What cheek! What nerve! And yet—just his very sauce made her want to smile. She turned abruptly from him and began spreading butter on bread. This was no smiling matter and, as he busied himself filling the kettle and plugging it in, she didn't want him in the kitchen either.

The kitchen had always appeared adequately sized before but, with him in it, there barely seemed room to breathe. He seemed much too close. Sabina concentrated on getting his salmon sandwich done and was just cutting it into neat quarters when— Good grief, what in creation was she doing? With a start she suddenly realised

she should be showing him the door, not feeding the
brute!

She turned, ready to let forth with something unwel-
coming—but only for the words to die in her throat. He
was too close. 'Have you had time to have your own
meal?' he enquired conversationally.

Those eyes—dark, penetrating. She turned from him
with no idea why she should suddenly start to feel confused. 'I had something to eat when I got in from the
office,' she stated, concentrating hard on the extra
sandwich she was making.

'What sort of work do you do?' he wanted to know
in passing.

Well, if it kept him off the subject of that ring it was
no hardship to answer him. 'Secretarial.'

'You enjoy it?'

'I've only been with this firm a few weeks.' She saw
no point in telling him that previously she had worked
for her father. Let him think that she changed jobs every
five minutes. 'So far it seems very interesting.' She finished making him a plate of sandwiches and, on the 'if
you can't beat 'em, join 'em' principle, made two cups
of coffee.

'What sort of work do they do?'

'Who?'

'The firm you work for.'

Sabina put the sandwiches and coffee on a tray. There
was fishing and fishing. She looked Yorke Mackinnon
in the eye and in answer to the question he was really
asking told him, 'I work for Alpha Computers.'

He grinned; her knees went weak. 'Allow me,' he offered, and took up the tray and carried it into the sitting
room.

Sabina took a moment out to get herself together again
before she followed. Grief, what was it about this man?
He had placed the tray down on a small table when she

joined him, but was courteously waiting for her before he availed himself of a chair.

'Take a seat,' she suggested, and realised she quite liked his manners when he waited for her to sit down first before taking his own chair.

She did not care for his questions, though, when, having devoured one sandwich and selecting another, he casually remarked, 'You don't have a steady boyfriend?' Sabina sent him a sharp look. 'You were home last night and you're home again tonight,' he murmured by way of explanation.

And she wanted to kill him. Failing that, she wanted him to finish his sandwiches and clear off—he made it sound as if she was some plain Jane wallflower whom nobody wanted!

'I have my offers!' she replied snappily, wishing with all she had that she had accepted Chris Dawson's invitation out that night.

'But you're choosy?'

Really, this man! 'How about yourself?' she enquired. He could have had a date after he'd left here last night, and could have something arranged for later this evening, she realised. It was still comparatively early. 'You're not going steady?' she queried, but, remembering, quickly added, 'Oh, I forgot—you're not thinking of giving up your freedom.'

'We weren't talking about me,' he hinted.

Tough! 'You and Rod are cousins, I think you said?'

He downed his coffee, eyed her silently for some moments, and, she guessed, decided, for the moment, to play it her way. 'Our mothers were sisters.'

'Rod's parents were killed in a car accident a couple of years ago, I believe,' she checked, starting to wonder what other lies Rod might have told Natalie.

'They were,' Yorke confirmed, and while Sabina thought what had happened to Rod's parents was a terrible tragedy it was a relief to know that, about that, he had been speaking the truth.

She glanced across at her 'guest's' empty coffee-cup, and felt more relief. The sandwiches were gone too. 'I see you've finished your coffee,' she prompted, preparing to stand up prior to seeing him out.

'Thank you,' he replied, not budging. And, all pretence slipping away, he suggested politely, 'And now, if I may, I'd like to see the ring.'

Damn and blast him! Suddenly, like a thunderclap, she only then realised that his smiles, his grin, his charm had all been part and parcel of a calculated attempt to cool her anger, to get her mellow, soften her up, before he got down to the nitty-gritty of his sole purpose in being there—to relieve her of that ring.

She stood up. 'I'll send you a photo!' she answered bluntly.

He was not best pleased, and was on his feet too, clearly very annoyed with her. Great—he wasn't her most favourite person either. 'Look here—I'm a busy man,' he began curtly.

'My time's valuable too!' she retorted.

'Then you'll agree that it's pointless our wasting time in arguing over an item which, until I've seen it, might well not be the same ring that my grandmother gave to me to hold.'

He was right there, of course. But just the fact of him being in the right—which therefore made her the one in the wrong—niggled Sabina. 'Nobody asked you to argue in the first place,' she tossed at him belligerently, and, getting well and truly wound up, 'And I've got better things to do too than spend my life making you salmon sandwiches!'

A minuscule movement of his lips caused her to think she had caught at his sense of humour, but he refused to smile. And then that moment of a stray strand of amusement seeming to touch him at her acid was gone and he was all aggression.

Manfully, however, it seemed he swallowed down his mighty irritation with her, and instead of serving her a helping of something short, sharp and totally unwanted he took a controlling breath. And, clearly against his better judgement, causing Sabina to realise, if she had not realised before, that he was a man who explained nothing to anyone, he began, 'I've told you that that ring belongs to my grandmother. What I haven't told you...' he paused, and Sabina filled in the unsaid words—because it's none of your business—'...is that she only gave me the ring—which incidentally is a favourite of hers and one which she always wears—while in hospital about to undergo major heart surgery.'

'Oh!' Sabina exclaimed softly, all her antipathy to this man melting away. But that was before it quickly dawned on her that this man was after Natalie's engagement ring and, being as tough as she judged him, would not care what tales he told in order to get his hands on it. And in the next instant she was hardening her heart against him and any other softening-up stories he might have up his sleeve. 'You've just invented that!' she charged hostilely.

'Believe me, I haven't,' he denied.

Sabina stared at him, her large brown eyes trying to gauge if he was telling the truth. 'But why give it to you?' she asked in spite of herself. 'Why not Rod? You as good as stated not ten minutes ago that he's a grandson too.'

Yorke Mackinnon eyed her for some moments. Then, with a brief shrug, 'Work it out for yourself,' he suggested.

'Sentimental reasons?' she attempted. 'She loves you more than she loves him? No accounting for taste!' she mumbled under her breath.

My, he had sharp ears! She knew he had heard her mumbled last comment when those dark, penetrating eyes stared down at her, before a moment later she most definitely saw his superb mouth twitch—as though she had again amused him.

But his expression was void of any such amusement when he answered, 'No.' Just that, and no more.

'Then why—?' She broke off, staring at him, that 'why' eluding her as she tried, as he'd suggested, to work it out for herself. She found she could come up with little. Little, that was, until she remembered how last night he had aggressively asked her if Rod had sold the ring. 'Your grandmother thought he might *sell* it?' she gasped.

Yorke returned her look steadily. 'Other items have gone.'

'He stole other items of jewellery?' she asked faintly, feeling sick inside. Oh, poor Natalie!

'Not stole,' Yorke answered. 'My grandmother gave him Grandfather's gold watch and cuff-links.'

'And he sold them?'

'They were then his to sell.'

'But your grandmother didn't like it—and didn't want to trust him with a ring that was a favourite and had been in the family for such a long time.'

'That's about it,' he agreed. 'So you see, Rod never did own that ring which he gave your friend when he asked her to be engaged to him.'

Sabina stared at him silently, not quite sure when it was that she had started to believe this man's word above that of his cousin, Natalie's fiancé— Oh, grief, what a mess. She wished Natalie were there. Oh, how she wished that.

'It's only your word against Rod's,' loyalty to her friend and the man Natalie loved made her assert. Oh, heavens, Yorke Mackinnon wasn't liking it. 'And there's

no way I'm going to meekly hand it over just like that,'
she further maintained, and cared not at all for the look
of taut anger on his face. 'Anyway,' she went on swiftly
as she recalled him telling her that his grandmother had
given him the ring to hold, 'since by the very act of giving
the ring into your safekeeping your grandmother trusts
you, surely she'll trust you a little while longer until
Natalie and Rod come home.'

That hadn't gone down well either, she noted, but she
defiantly stood her ground. Now, above all other times—
with Natalie so in love with a man who at the least had
lied to her—she must support her, be there for her—and
that included not handing over that ring just on this
man's say-so.

Like warring combatants they stared at each other.
But, just when it seemed Yorke Mackinnon might let fly
with something guaranteed to wound, he changed his
mind, and as if realising he was getting nowhere, and
clearly against what he would like to do, decided,
'Perhaps I should explain more fully the reason my
grandmother wanted me to hold onto the ring for her.'

It wasn't going to make a scrap of difference. 'Perhaps
you should,' Sabina answered nicely.

He was not deceived by her suddenly sweet manner,
she could tell; she'd hardly expected that he would be.
But doggedly he ploughed on. 'Eight days ago, the
Sunday before my grandmother's operation on the
Monday, I went to the hospital to see her.'

'Oh, yes,' Sabina commented noncommittally.

'Rod turned up to see her too.'

'That would be Sunday morning?' Sabina put in—
Rod had been with Natalie in the afternoon and evening.

Yorke nodded. 'Though just before Rod arrived my
grandmother had been confiding her fears that she wasn't
going to make it through the operation.' Sabina had no
chance of hanging onto her feelings of hostility, but

before she could offer any sympathetic comment he was continuing, 'Naturally I tried to assure her that she would come sailing through, but she wasn't having any of it and at that point took off the ring and told me to give it to the woman I wanted to marry.'

Oh, heavens, his grandmother had given him the ring to hold not because of some fear of burglary, as she had first thought might be the case, but because she feared she was not going to survive major heart surgery!

'I . . .' Sabina gasped helplessly.

And had her soft heart further pummelled when Yorke went on, 'She was very distressed, so much so that the only way I could think to calm her was to take the ring from her.'

'Which you did.'

'Which I did,' he confirmed. 'While at the same time I gave my solemn word that I would return it the moment her doctors told me that she was out of danger and on the way to making a good recovery. She insisted *only* then.'

'Don't . . .' Sabina begged.

He ignored her, and pressed toughly on. 'So unless I have that ring to return to her she will think the worst— that she hasn't long to—'

'Stop . . .' Sabina pleaded; she didn't want to hear any more.

'For the first few days after her operation my grand-mother was barely aware of anything going on around her. But since Friday she has been more aware and, while I might mention that prior to this she has always been a very strong, positive lady, where once she was always cheerful regardless of what trials she had to bear she is now more often tearful and—'

'That would be the result of the operation, the an-aesthetic,' Sabina interrupted quickly, not knowing the first thing about it, but wanting reasons, excuses. Yorke

Mackinnon was ruthlessly battering down her defences—and Natalie *had* to come first. 'Anyhow...' She lunged away from thoughts of his poor, still seriously ill grandmother—if she'd only recently had her operation. 'Anyhow, how come you let Rod steal the ring from you? For all I know it could have been Rod to whom your grandmother gave that ring and said to give it to the woman he wanted to marry. It—'

'It could have been, but it wasn't,' Yorke cut in shortly. 'He saw it in my hand when he came in to visit our grandmother. I slipped it into my pocket and said my goodbyes and left them. I went to have a word with the head nurse, and was in the hospital car park when Rod caught up with me—his car was in the garage for some problem and he wanted a lift. I—'

'He...' Sabina butted in, and halted.

'He?' Yorke wanted more—and Sabina started to feel defiant again.

'If you must know, his car wasn't in any garage with any problem—Rod sold it.'

'Sold it?' his cousin echoed.

'Sold it—to finance his trip with Natalie and,' she added triumphantly, 'to enable him to purchase Natalie's engagement ring.'

'Huh!' Yorke scoffed. 'Well, we've established one thing: my cousin Rodney was lying to one of us.'

'How do I know that you're not the one who's lying?'

'You're still refusing to believe me?'

'Give me one good reason why I should.'

'How about I've got a very sick and worried grandmother lying in hospital for one?'

That was below the belt. 'So how come Rod managed to steal that ring from you? How long was he in your car?'

'Long enough,' was the terse reply.

'He picked your pocket?' she enquired, her scepticism showing.

'Precisely that!' he answered curtly. 'As Rod suggested, to drop him off here at his girlfriend Natalie's place wasn't far off my route if I was going from the hospital to my own home.'

'You dropped him off here last Sunday?' So that was how Yorke Mackinnon had known where Natalie lived— and where his cousin might be found when yesterday he had come looking for him!

'I did,' he agreed. 'But first I had to stop for petrol on the way. I'd tossed my jacket on the back seat and—'

'And the ring wasn't there when you came back,' she quickly caught on.

But Yorke shook his head. 'I didn't check then. It was only yesterday, after a visit to the hospital, that I realised just how much the operation had weakened my grandmother, sapped her fight and made her nervous. Sabina,' he said sternly, 'if I don't return that ring to her she'll lose all will and start to believe her fears...'

'That the operation wasn't successful,' Sabina finished for him.

He did not confirm it. He had no need to. 'I've searched every inch of my car on the remote chance that the ring fell from my pocket. It's not there. So now,' he went on heavily, 'I'd be obliged if you'd show me the ring that my cousin gave to your friend Natalie.'

'I...' she began, her thoughts with his poor sick grandmother. Oh, heavens... But suddenly her thoughts lighted on her dear friend too. Natalie, who had never harmed anyone in her life. And Sabina pulled herself up short. For all Yorke Mackinnon looked and sounded sincere, and with his wealth he had no need to try and con her into giving the ring to him, he could be lying. 'I'm not going to give it to you!' she told him bluntly

as she hung on grimly to one thought—that she was not
going to let Natalie down.

Oh, help. Rod's cousin had been looking none too
sweet before; he was looking positively murderous now
as he threw her a malevolent look and grated, 'I know
that!' She guessed he must have been counting to a re-
straining ten then, because somehow he managed to
control his frustration at her stubbornness, to go on to
explain crisply, carefully, 'What I'm saying is that in the
event that all my surmises are wrong, and my cousin did
not steal his grandmother's ring from me to give to his
lady-love, then I have to somehow find out where it is
so I can try to get it back before it's sold on.'

Sabina understood perfectly well what he was saying,
and her sensitivities were pulled all ways. By the sound
of it, once that ring was back on his grandmother's hand,
she would begin to fight and not give in to how poorly
she must be feeling at this time. But Sabina did not care
at all for Yorke calling Natalie his cousin's 'lady-love'.
It had a derogatory sound to it—and Natalie was worth
better than that. As too she was worth better than that
she should be in love with a man who would steal what
should be a symbol of his sincerity of intent—and then
break that sincerity by telling her he had purposely purchased the engagement ring.

Looking at Yorke Mackinnon, facing his steady, un-
wavering dark-eyed gaze which seemed to be telling the
truth, Sabina knew then that she too had to know the
truth about that wretched ring.

'Wait here,' she said stiffly, and left him to go to
Natalie's bedroom.

She closed the bedroom door, and did not like what
she was doing. But she was uncertain what to believe
any more. If Natalie's ring was not the ring in question
and if Yorke Mackinnon was as truthful as he seemed,
then he would tell her that he had made a mistake in

thinking his cousin a thief. He would then bid her goodnight and she would never see him again, and she would
go back to being happy in the belief that Natalie had
fallen in love, this time with someone she could trust.

Sabina, keeping a nervous eye on the door lest Yorke
Mackinnon should follow her and attempt to take the
ring from her, opened her friend's wardrobe and retrieved it, and with that precious item gripped firmly in
her palm she went back to the sitting room.

Yorke Mackinnon was standing exactly where she had
left him. Standing with barely concealed impatience,
waiting to see the item of jewellery which was his sole
reason for being there.

Impatiently he held out his hand to inspect the ring.
And, indeed, there was such an air of authority about
him that Sabina almost gave it to him.

Her breath caught and hastily, childishly, she realised,
and not liking to again feel a fool, she put her hands
behind her back, instinctively pushing the ring onto one
of her fingers for further security.

His look of impatience became one of exasperation,
and, wondering what she was scared of—he was hardly
likely to break a few of her fingers in an attempt to snatch
the ring from her— Sabina brought her left hand from
behind her back and held it out for his inspection.

'Is this the one?' she asked, feeling a mite confused,
she had to own, when he caught hold of the tips of her
fingers to bring her hand up for inspection. Her skin
tingled, but even as he nodded, a glance all he needed
to confirm that it was indeed the ring his grandmother
always wore and had given him to hold, she was realising that there was an inner quality about him that
would never allow him to use physical violence on a
woman.

With her fingers intact, not a break to be seen, the
ring still on one of them, he let go of her fingertips.

Sabina's eyes went from her hand and up to his face—where she all at once observed that an alert look had come to those dark blue eyes. He even seemed to rock back on his heels slightly, but, watching him, Sabina was certain there was a speculative look about him. She was positive his sharp mind was sifting through something, when he drawled, 'Now isn't that one hell of an idea.'

'What?' Clearly something had just struck him.

He did not answer at once, but mulled over whatever idea had just come to him for a few moments, before questioning, 'You're still maintaining you aren't going to allow me to return that ring to its rightful owner?'

How could she? 'I've only your word that your grandmother is the rightful owner,' she mumbled, suddenly feeling quite dreadful. Natalie's idol did, it seemed, have feet of clay. She swallowed hard at the injustice of it all, and just had to tell him, 'Everybody's always letting Natalie down—I just can't do it.'

'I admire your loyalty!' he clipped curtly, in a tone that said he did nothing of the kind. He then let go a very fed-up-sounding breath, and was all authoritative again when he decreed, 'That settles it. We'll have to do that!'

'Do *what*?' she asked, mystified. *We*?

He nodded down to the ring she wore—the only ring she wore. 'It fits your engagement finger,' he pointed out.

She hadn't realised that she had slipped it onto that finger of her left hand. 'My fingers are smaller than Natalie's,' she told him for no good reason.

'And you're definitely not going to let me have that ring?' he enquired again.

He seemed to be more accepting of it now, she thought, and with quite a huge slice of relief she was able to reiterate, 'Most definitely not.'

Only for her relief to shoot away on a rocket-propelled ejector seat when calmly, unhurriedly, he authoritatively told her, 'Then you'd better be wearing it on that finger when you come with me to the hospital tomorrow to visit my grandmother.'

Her mouth fell open. Incapable of speech, she just stood and looked at him. 'Wh... I'm not...' She was too amazed to be able to form any of the denials, the sentences, the questions that rushed to her lips.

Not that he was waiting for her to recover, however, for, with a glance to his watch as if to suggest that she had already taken up too much of his time, he outlined, 'I've told you that my grandmother gave me that ring requesting that I give it to the woman I want to marry. I, for my part, have promised to return that ring to her only when I know she's on the way to making a full recovery.' He took an impatient breath, and then said, looking for all the world as if he meant it, 'With you being so bloody-minded about not handing it over, the only way I can see to show her she has nothing to worry about is to take that ring to her—on the engagement finger of my fiancée—the woman I want to marry.'

Sabina stared at him. Blinked, and stared again. He could not seriously be serious! She opened her mouth to tell him so. No sound came. Breathless, utterly staggered, she could only stare wordlessly at him.

CHAPTER THREE

'B-BUT...' Sabina spluttered, still staring at him incredulously as what he'd said and meant started to register more fully in her mind. 'I can't do that!' she gasped.

'You've got something against hospitals?' Yorke Mackinnon questioned—for all the world as if he thought it was hospital visiting that she objected to rather than his assertion—for it was not a request but more of an order—that she go to visit his grandmother with him and play the part of the woman he intended to marry.

'Don't be so deliberately obtuse!' Sabina retorted hotly, fear that this man might browbeat her into so unthinkable an act making her jumpy. 'You know I don't mean the hospital!'

'Then what's your objection?' His eyes had narrowed at her tone, at her refusal to at once comply with his idea—his totally ridiculous idea, she fumed—but his tone, for all that, was reasonable, and every bit as if he could not for the life of him see what she was objecting to.

He really did bring out the worst in her, Sabina realised, because sarcasm—a tool she hadn't known she possessed in such acid measure before meeting him—was there again when, with no small degree of arrogance of her own, she enlightened him, 'Whilst you seem to believe that half the female population in London would give their eye-teeth for the chance of being engaged to you, and, while it grieves me more than I can say to dent your ego, I, Mr Mackinnon, am not one of them!'

For several seconds he eyed her coolly. Then, when
Sabina felt sure that something sharp and stinging was
coming her way, suddenly, and totally disarmingly, he
smiled. The effect was weakening. Her temper started
to dip. 'It would only be for one visit,' he suggested per-
suasively—and, totally against what she wanted, she
began to feel inexplicably mean for not having agreed
straight away.

'I—couldn't do it,' she stressed, seeming then to need
to impress that fact on herself as much as on him.

'Yes, you could,' he contradicted mildly.

'I couldn't,' she denied. 'I'm no good at telling lies—
I'd slip up.'

'No, you wouldn't,' he answered, calm where she was
agitated. 'Besides, I'd be there. Any small problem and
I'd cover you.'

'No,' she refused.

'You wouldn't have to visit for long,' he ignored her
refusal. 'Just a few minutes—wearing the ring, of
course.'

'I'm not going!' Sabina told him forthrightly, wishing
she felt as determined about that as she sounded. She
fished around for some kind of strong argument, thought
she found it, and went on to challenge, 'Anyhow, what's
to stop me telling your grandmother the truth—that you
and I aren't engaged, that—?'

Yorke Mackinnon cut her short, a tough, no-nonsense
light glinting in his eyes. 'You'd tell her that the ring she
gave to me was stolen by my cousin—her other
grandson?' he clipped. Oh, Lord, what a mess! 'You *do*
know that the reason my grandmother is in hospital is
because of her heart condition?'

'Damn you!' Sabina snapped frustratedly, not needing
him to go on—it would probably kill the elderly and sick
lady to know that her grandson Rodney was a thief.
'What time tomorrow?'

'You say,' he invited with barely a pause—as if there had never been any uncertainty that she would go with him. And Sabina glared at him—having got her agreement, he no doubt felt he could afford to be magnanimous.

Sabina started to walk to the outer door. This had gone on long enough. She needed space, wanted to think. 'It had better be straight after work. Your grandmother won't want to be bothered with visitors late in the evening. I'll go to the hospital straight from the office. Which one is it?'

She was glad to close the door on him. But, having agreed to meet him at six o'clock, within a few minutes of his departure she was wishing that she had never agreed to anything so outrageous! Good heavens, what on earth had she been thinking of? She just wasn't a liar! In fact she was absolutely useless when it came to telling lies. And yet here she was prepared to lie to some elderly person she had never before met, even to the extent of wearing a ring on her finger to back that lie up.

On that instant Sabina went to Natalie's room and returned the ring to where she had taken it from. Oh, how she wished that Natalie were back!

But Natalie had more or less only just gone, and Sabina went to bed worrying about her and the man Natalie was engaged to, and wishing she had never seen his cousin. And most heartily wishing that she had never been so weak as to give Yorke Mackinnon her word that she would meet him at the hospital tomorrow.

She slept badly and guessed it was her guilty conscience that was responsible for that. But—what else could she do? She had half a mind to ring Yorke Mackinnon come morning and tell him she had changed her mind. But that still left one very sick old lady in hospital with a true-to-his-word grandson having solemnly promised her he would only return her ring to her when he was sure she was going to pull through. So how could she not go and visit her?

How could she not go and show her that the only reason Yorke was not returning the ring to her was that he, under his grandmother's instruction, had given it to the woman he wanted to marry?

Sabina was up at first light, knowing that the obvious answer was for her to hand over that ring to Yorke Mackinnon and that would be the end of it. But how could she hand the ring over? It didn't belong to her for one thing. It belonged to Natalie. And all Natalie wanted was to be loved, and people were always letting Natalie down.

She went to work still worrying about the predicament which—without even trying—she seemed to have got herself in. But at eleven-fifteen that morning she had Yorke Mackinnon and the whole ghastly nightmare briefly taken from her thoughts when Chris Dawson came to her office. Whereupon she discovered that any passing notion she might have had that, having refused Chris's invitation to go out with him last night, he would not ask her out again was very much misplaced.

Indeed, he seemed keener than ever when he smiled winningly and enquired, 'You were busy last night; I refuse to believe you can't find a small space for me for this evening.'

'I'm afraid I'm—er—hospital visiting tonight, Chris,' she smiled, and, having refused his invitation out a second time, Yorke Mackinnon's 'You were home last night and you're home again tonight' played back in her ears. 'But I could meet you later if you like,' she offered.

'We'll have dinner,' he at once snatched at her offer. 'What time will you be free? I'll pick you up at the hospital if you like.'

'I'll be in my own car,' she told Chris, and suggested, 'You tell me where, and I'll drive...'

Chris did not care for that idea, it seemed. 'This is my date. Tell me where you live and I'll come by your home and pick you up,' he counter-suggested, and with an eager grin asked, 'What time?'

Sabina calculated that she would be away from the hospital well before six-thirty. Seven, at the very outside. 'Is eight o'clock too late?' she asked, to be on the safe side.

'I'll be there,' he promised.

It would do her good to go out, Sabina decided. It would do her good to have something else to think about besides Yorke Mackinnon and that wretched, wretched ring. Oh, how she wished that she had never given in and agreed to visit his grandmother in hospital.

Thoughts of Yorke Mackinnon and his plan to deceive his grandparent—albeit in a very good cause—were still playing on her mind in the early afternoon. Then suddenly she realised that incredibly, when she had thought of very little else, she had not brought the dratted ring she was to wear with her to the office.

Freud would have had something to say about it, she was sure. It was as if, with everything honest in her crying out against that which she was about to do, her subconscious had blotted out the necessity of temporarily borrowing that which one cousin said belonged to his grandmother but which the other cousin had said he had sold his car to purchase. And which, at the end of the day, had to belong to her very dear friend, Natalie.

Sabina tried to get on with some work whilst at the same time she realised, frustratedly, that since the whole point of her going to the hospital at all was to show the ring on her hand she was first going to have to detour out of her way to go home and collect it.

Even as that thought landed she was reaching for her bag and for the card inside it that would remind her of Yorke Mackinnon's direct-line business number. Next, she reached for the phone.

'Louise Page,' answered a calm voice she recognised from yesterday.

'Oh, hello—is Yorke available?'

'I'm afraid he's out all afternoon. May I—?'

'No—no, it's fine.' Sabina cut off what she was sure would be an invitation to take a message.

There was nothing for it—she was going to be late. He'd love that, wouldn't he? She doubted that anyone ever kept *him* waiting. She toyed, but only briefly, with the idea of not going to the hospital at all—and doubted anyone had ever stood him up either. But, remembering the man, the tough look of him when he wasn't minded to be pleasant, Sabina felt that, rather than having him ringing her doorbell champing to give her a talking-to for breaking her word, a visit to the hospital—as much as she did not want to go—was the better of the two options.

She appreciated punctuality in others, and was invariably punctual herself. Which made her consider that Freud would have had his work cut out with her that day. Because, having left her office a little after five and driven back to her flat, and having retrieved Natalie's engagement ring, she found she was delaying in going out to her car again.

Her reluctance was perfectly understandable, she felt. And, since she was going out to dinner later, surely it was equally perfectly understandable that, just in case she was in a rush getting back, she delayed a few more minutes and changed now? Since it had been a hot, sweltering summer's day, the quickest of showers wouldn't hurt either.

Half an hour later, and dressed in a linen two-piece of the palest lemon, Sabina was ready to leave the apartment. Then the phone rang. She was in two minds whether or not to answer it. But, with hope in her heart that—even at this late stage—Yorke Mackinnon might be ringing to call it off, she delayed further to answer it.

'Hello?' she enquired on picking up the instrument.

'I thought I'd ring now, because I'm going out later.' It was her mother.

It was another ten minutes before Sabina went out to her car. She always enjoyed having a chat to her parent but to tell her that she was in a hurry, and why, had been out of the question. Guilt that she was not able to be completely open with her mother had seen her agreeing to go to her old home in Surrey that weekend when she had half promised to give her old friend Oliver Robbins supper on Saturday evening. Perhaps he'd settle for Sunday.

There was no sign of Yorke Mackinnon hanging around the hospital car park when she got there. And as Sabina made her way inside the entrance of the plush private hospital so, with no sign of him in the comfortably furnished waiting lounge either, it suddenly dawned on her that if she was to enquire at Reception where she might find his grandmother, then it might be an idea if she had some clue as to his grandmother's name.

It wasn't Mackinnon, she knew that as she went forward to the reception desk. She clearly remembered Yorke telling her that his mother and Rod's mother had been sisters, but as to what their maiden name had been she hadn't a clue.

The receptionist looked up from the computer she had been busy with. Sabina plunged in, 'I'm visiting—' then

she broke off and tried again, 'I arranged to meet a Mr
Yorke Mackinnon here—I don't suppose he...?'

A brilliant smile was her reward. Clearly the receptionist knew full well who Mr Yorke Mackinnon was.
'He's with Mrs Fairfax at this very moment. Room 203,'
she added, and, any friend of Yorke Mackinnon a friend
of hers, apparently, she smilingly proceeded to give her
directions.

All too soon, given that she was all of three quarters
of an hour late, she arrived at the door of room 203.
She raised her hand to knock then at that late stage, not
wanting to go through with it, almost turned about and
went smartly out of there. She hesitated and as a vision
came to mind of Yorke Mackinnon camping out on her
doorstep demanding an explanation—or that she hand
over the ring that now adorned her engagement finger—
Sabina quickly tapped on the door and went in.

The receptionist had not lied. He was there. He had
been seated but left his chair by the bed the moment she
entered—and took over.

Sabina supposed she should have been grateful for
that. But she didn't quite know how she felt when,
halting close up to her, he placed his hands on her arms
and, the contact lasting a moment or two longer than
any conventional greeting should in her view, kissed her
fully on her mouth.

She was aware that she had a part to play. But, while
her heart suddenly started to thunder, she had the hardest
work not to push him away. This kiss was for his
watching grandmother's benefit.

At last, although in actual fact that kiss of greeting
had not been overly long, she realised, Yorke took his
mouth from hers. She looked up at him, guessing, since
the whole of her skin seemed to be burning, that her
cheeks must be tinged with pink.

His mouth, that superb mouth that had just brushed hers, was smiling. Superb! Hurriedly Sabina took her glance from his mouth, but the moment her eyes met the ice in his look so she knew that smile to be a misnomer.

'Just where in sweet hell have you been?' he demanded, his voice low—for all anyone a couple of yards away might have known he could have been whispering endearments.

Grief—and she'd thought he would come to the apartment demanding an explanation? From that arctic look in his eyes it was far more likely he'd have called to throttle her sooner.

'Traffic!' she murmured with a matching smile—she who had an inability to lie stepping effortlessly onto that downward conveyor belt.

She felt her hand caught in his, and heard genuine warmth in his tones when, turning her to face the bed where a white-haired, aristocratic, still beautiful elderly lady sat watching them, he said, 'Pebbie, I'd like you to meet another very special lady in my life—Sabina Constable. Sabina, come and say hello to my grandmother, Mrs Phoebe Fairfax.'

Sabina went forward, and while she loathed with all she had the deception they were playing on his frail-looking grandmother she all at once saw that there was no other way. Saw too that, while Yorke might hate like blazes the necessity to lie to this genteel-looking soul, if lying to her meant that she would regain her fighting spirit and so get well again—then so be it.

'How do you do?' Yorke's grandmother extended her hand, her voice as frail as her look.

'How are you, Mrs Fairfax?' Sabina gently enquired, and discovered that she had no need to wonder why Yorke had not, as she had imagined that he would, introduced her as his fiancée, for as she shook the hand his grandmother extended to her those faded blue eyes suddenly came alive.

'What's this?' she asked, her voice sharper, stronger all at once, her look all-searching, all-enquiring when, as if it was impossible not to notice the ring that had adorned her own hand all those years, she caught sight of her favourite ring on Sabina's left hand.

'Did I not say that I'd a surprise for you? One that I thought you'd like?' Yorke was there smoothly, non-urgently, saving Sabina from having to answer.

'You're—you're engaged?' Mrs Fairfax queried, light, life coming to her expression, even the blue of her eyes seeming to deepen.

'I know I should have given the ring back to you,' Yorke answered, 'but you said to give it to the woman I wanted to marry and, well...' He took his look from his grandmother and, smiling at Sabina, said, 'And you fell in love with it, didn't you, darling?'

'Do you mind very much?' Sabina asked chokily, well and truly a part of this whole lie now, although in the face of the joy that was growing and growing, the life that was coming back to this woman who, at somewhere in her early seventies, Sabina judged, had just been through major heart surgery, she suddenly felt able to lie her head off if that was what was needed to set her on the path to a full recovery.

'My dear, I'm delighted,' Phoebe Fairfax beamed, her sincerity obvious, it seemed to Sabina, as she turned to congratulate her grandson, to sit up straighter in her bed, her blue eyes now matching the warm blue of her smart satin bed jacket. And, after some moments of beaming smiles and emotion, she turned to include Sabina happily. 'When are you planning to marry?' Sabina was hard put to it to keep a smile on her face but she could only watch, fascinated, when Yorke Mackinnon, totally unperturbed, dealt with that very leading question.

'Not until you're out of here and recovered enough to be able to attend both the wedding and wedding breakfast,' he smiled cheerfully.

'But that could take—ages!' his grandmother protested.

'And, having seen Sabina for yourself, you'll know I'm impatient to make her Mrs Mackinnon,' he returned, and Sabina watched, stunned—he hadn't been joking when he'd said any small problem and he'd cover for her. 'So...'

'So I'd better buck my ideas up,' his grandmother finished for him.

A short while after that and Yorke was telling his grandparent that he thought she'd had enough excitement for one day. And Sabina suddenly saw that perhaps meeting her grandson's 'fiancée' had done more to make the elderly lady feel better than if Yorke had returned the ring to her.

She was by then uncertain about how she herself felt about any of it, but was able to wish Phoebe Fairfax a warm goodbye, and, hoping she would think she was leaving a few minutes ahead of her fiancé in case she needed to have a few private words with him, Sabina left the flower-filled room.

She had not reached the end of the short corridor, however, when, any satisfying thought that, her mission accomplished, that was the last she would see of Yorke Mackinnon, he caught up with her—his long strides eating up the ground.

Sabina had thought he could have not the smallest complaint to make. Everything had gone swimmingly. She was wrong. 'I didn't think you were coming!' he snarled with singular lack of charm.

So—she'd been forty-five minutes late! She had no excuse—clearly he had not swallowed her 'traffic' reason for being late. 'Just be grateful I came at all!' she snapped as they left the building and walked to the car park.

'Working late?' He refused to leave it alone. Plainly he must have hung around in the hospital lounge waiting for her to turn up. My stars, she'd bet he'd been seething!

As if she cared! 'I went home to...' She found she had begun to explain anyway. Abruptly, she stopped. Oddly she discovered that she did not want him to know how all at once disorganised, mixed up her head had become. That when her only reason for her agreeing to go straight from her office to the hospital had been to display that ring she had forgotten completely to take that item to the office with her. Sabina halted by her car. He halted too, his expression grim as, clearly waiting for her to finish what she had started to say, he looked down at her. 'I—I went home to change!' she told him crisply.

And did not know whether to be furious or whether to laugh when, his look softening, he commented, 'That was thoughtful of you.' Then, his absent charm back in full force, he went on to decree, 'You're forgiven,' and, a smile playing about his mouth, said, 'I'll buy you a salmon sandwich.'

The sauce of it! She wouldn't laugh. 'I didn't change for you!' she let him know in no uncertain terms. 'I've a dinner date—so you can keep your sal—'

'The hell you have!' he cut in, fury instant, before she could tell him what he could do with his salmon sandwich. 'Wearing my ring!'

She glared at him, his fury causing her own anger to rocket. Honestly—this man! 'Here, have your wretched ring!' she hissed, and had pulled the ring half off her finger ready to hurl at him when some sense of what she was doing landed. Good heavens, this wasn't about her and him! It wasn't even a ring he had given to her. It belonged to Natalie! Hastily, sparks flashing in her eyes for all that she felt panicky at what she had so nearly done, she rammed the ring home again.

'*You!*' she raged.

And was all mixed up again when, his fury dying as quickly as it had been born, he stared down into her fire-filled large brown eyes and conceded, 'My grandmother was right.'

'About what?' Sabina flared, not sure that she couldn't cope better with his fury than with this quiet, sort of assessing mood.

'You are beautiful,' he remarked easily—he could have been talking about the weather!

'Your grandmother said that?' Sabina found she was questioning just the same.

'She did.'

'When?' she challenged—there'd barely been any time after she'd left for him to have any sort of conversation with Mrs Fairfax, Sabina decided. Yorke must have more or less followed her from his grandmother's room.

'She told me as I bent to kiss her goodbye.'

Sabina wished she had not asked. Talking of kisses reminded her that not a half-hour ago Yorke Mackinnon had placed his mouth over hers—it had not been un-pleasant. Swiftly she made herself think of his grand-mother—and she straight away wished that she had not. For, in doing so, in remembering that aristocratic, satin-bed-jacketed figure, she remembered also her look of frailty, the very serious heart surgery she had recently undergone—and Sabina was weakened.

So much so, she discovered she was trying to excuse her actions. 'Look, Yorke,' she began, having had no intention of using his first name, his name just sort of slipping out. 'Look,' she went on hurriedly, 'you know I can't let you have this ring. But the moment Natalie comes back—or before if she phones and agrees after

she's heard what I have to say—I'll return it to you.'
There, she couldn't be fairer than that, could she?

She rather thought Yorke thought so too, for his look
on her seemed to soften for a moment or two. But any
seeming softening in him was an illusion—for a moment
later he was biting her head off.

'And you think *I've* got a nerve!' he barked, and
wasted not another moment to remind her. 'That ring
doesn't belong to you—it belongs in my family!'

As before, he was again capable of arousing instant
anger in her. She objected to his bossy tone; she objected to him. There was no arguing with him.

'Oh, to hell with you!' she raged, and, unlocking her
car, opened the driver's door.

It seemed that Yorke Mackinnon was like-minded, and
felt that there was no arguing with her either. '*Bon appétit!*' he snarled, and, without so much as a glance at
her, strode angrily away to his car.

Sabina got behind the steering wheel of her car and
set the vehicle in motion, her sense of humour being
picked at by his parting remark. Yet, even so, she was
furious, and glanced across to see that Yorke had gone
to a sleek black car nearby.

Hastily she averted her head, suddenly aware that she
had a smile on her face. Damn him. Damn him, damn
him. Now why on earth was it that, even when she was
furious with him, he could make her smile?

CHAPTER FOUR

THE weather continued to hold fair, but Sabina spent the next few days in a far from sunny mood. And by the time Saturday arrived she knew without question that the ring which Rod Lacey had given Natalie was not a ring which he had purchased specially, as he had said.

'I know I should have given the ring back to you,' Yorke Mackinnon had told his grandmother. What better proof was there than that that the ring had not been Rod's to give to anybody? And yet, out of her love and loyalty to Natalie, Sabina still felt that she could not just hand it over. She could not let Natalie down that way. Yorke Mackinnon...

Sabina sat up; she didn't want to think of Yorke—she tried instead to concentrate her thoughts on Chris Dawson. Her dinner date with him last Tuesday had been quite enjoyable... Then Yorke Mackinnon was back again!

Perhaps, though, that was not so surprising after all, she mused as she left her bed and began her day. She had very strong views about dishonesty and since what she had been part and parcel of with Yorke had been out-and-out dishonesty—albeit in the most excellent of good causes—his grandmother's health—it was no wonder that he, the instigator of that dishonest deception, should be in her mind.

So, as enjoyable as her evening with Chris had been, it was no wonder either that thoughts of Yorke Mackinnon should arrive unheralded from time to time. She recalled how, even when furious with him, he could make her smile. Perverse sense of humour, she realised, recalling how his angry '*Bon appétit*' had caught at her sense of humour—for quite plainly he would by far, as she full well knew, have preferred that she choked on anything she ate.

She recalled Chris's 'Share the joke' comment as she'd chosen from the menu—and had realised she had been smiling again—and she'd had to make vigorous efforts to push one Yorke Mackinnon out of her head.

Sabina showered and dressed, recalling too how Chris had been waiting outside her apartment when she had returned from the hospital on Tuesday. How it had only been as she was getting out of her car that she'd noticed she still had that ring on her engagement finger. With no idea when it had become so comfortable that she had been able to forget she was wearing the wretched though beautiful thing, she'd hastily transferred it to her other hand. It had been around about then that she'd begun to recognise that since she had met Yorke Mackinnon she seemed to have changed from a non-deceiving, calm and well organised person into an emotional, over-excited disorganised person—who was often angry, not to mention mutinous, into the bargain.

Oh, for heaven's sake! Annoyed with herself that Yorke seemed to be forever in her head, Sabina made firmer efforts to put him from her mind. And yet he was somehow there again when she mused how when Chris Dawson had attempted to kiss her on the mouth she had turned her head away and his goodnight kiss had landed on her cheek. And it had had nothing whatsoever to do with the fact that Yorke, not so many hours earlier, had kissed her on the mouth. Of course it hadn't!

This was crazy! Why, she was never going to see him again—ever—thank goodness. Now do something constructive. Sabina went over to the phone and dialled her old friend Oliver Robbins.

'I was still in bed!' he complained.

'You should be ashamed of yourself—it's a beautiful morning,' she responded heartlessly, but added, her voice warming in friendship, 'Actually, I'm ringing to tell you I've decided to go and see my parents this weekend, and—'

'You mean I've got to wait until tomorrow to get fed properly!' he interrupted as it dawned on him that Sabina was putting off their supper semi-arrangement until the following evening.

'If you didn't want to live out of tins, you should never have left home,' she teased unsympathetically.

'If your mother offers to give you one of her delicious apple pies to bring back, don't refuse it,' he pleaded.

Sabina spent a quiet time in Surrey with her parents and returned to the apartment after lunch on Sunday. She decided a pasta dish might go some way to filling Oliver's lanky frame, and, although not very hungry herself, spent a pleasant evening with him, hearing about his latest pursuits and about Melissa—a young woman of his acquaintance.

On Monday Chris Dawson asked her to go out with him the following evening. 'I'm sorry,' she apologised.

'Thursday, then?' he questioned hopefully.

Oh, grief! Why was she being difficult? She quite liked him. 'I've saved Saturday for you,' she smiled, and found she was half hoping he was busy and couldn't make Saturday.

'Terrific,' he grinned—and she kept a smile on her face—and wondered what in creation was the matter with her.

The following few days passed uneventfully, but on Friday Sabina received a card from Natalie—a pretty near ecstatic card from Natalie—saying how marvellous everything was and how, by the time she received the card, she and Rod would be in Brazil.

It was lovely to hear from Natalie, lovely that she was so wonderfully happy. But it became a nagging source of worry to Sabina that, the ring Rod had given Natalie clearly belonging to his grandmother, there was no way in which she could save her friend from the hurt of finding that out. The least of it being that Rod had lied to her when he'd said he had sold his car to pay for it.

Sabina got ready to go out with Chris Dawson on Saturday with thoughts of Natalie, more than likely doing something adventurous up the Amazon, in her head, and, strangely, thoughts of Yorke Mackinnon—no doubt with some sophisticated beauty on his arm—embarking on some equally exciting evening niggling away at her.

Good grief, she scoffed, she was going to have an exciting evening too, wasn't she? Which was why she could not help but feel guilty because somehow, and she felt dreadful that it was so, a night out with Chris did not seem nearly as exciting as it once had.

Her date with Chris that evening was pleasant. He again tried to kiss her. And she again did not want him to, and averted her face. He suggested they go out next Tuesday but she felt that was too soon. Then, when he said something about their spending the day together on the next Saturday, stumped for an answer, she was not quick enough to find an excuse.

In consequence, she spent most of the week that followed trying to avoid him. By Friday she just knew he was going to corner her at some time during that day. But, while she knew that she did not want to go out with him again, she had nothing against him, and did not want to hurt his feelings. Nor, having once entered the field of deception, did she ever want to lie or deceive again. What she needed was a reason, a good and truthful reason she could give him.

Fate—cruel, wicked fate—was lurking to make a non-sense of what she wanted or did not want. At three-thirty that afternoon the phone on her desk rang. 'Hello?' she answered, and was absolutely dumbfounded to hear Yorke Mackinnon's grandmother on the other end of the phone!

'Phoebe Fairfax,' she announced, her voice sounding stronger than the last time Sabina had heard it. 'I'm sorry to ring you at your office,' she apologised while Sabina sought frantically to gather her scattered wits. 'Yorke told me where you worked—I hope you don't mind, but I don't have your home number.'

'Of course I don't mind,' Sabina replied, totally at a loss to know why the dear lady was ringing her; but, remembering how frail Mrs Fairfax had looked when she had visited her in hospital, she asked warmly, 'How are you, Mrs Fairfax?'

'As Yorke will have told you, I'm out of hospital now.'

'Oh, yes. Yes, he did,' Sabina found she was per-juring her soul yet again. She felt she should add some-thing—but what? She couldn't ask how long Mrs Fairfax had been out of hospital—she was supposed to know that!

'With Yorke away, though—' his grandmother saved her from asking anything which might make a nonsense of the whole deception— 'I couldn't help wondering if you were perhaps a little bit lonely.'

Yorke was away! Barely had that sunk in before Sabina was realising that what Mrs Fairfax was really saying was that she herself was feeling lonely now that her grandson was away. Her heart went out to her. The poor dear had recently been through so much.

'I do—er—tend to stay in a lot,' Sabina responded carefully. She had always been fairly happy with her own company, and there were endless places one could visit without feeling the need of an escort.

'So, at the moment, do I,' came the reply, and again Sabina's emotions were pricked. She was in the middle of envisaging the courageous woman stuck at home, still recovering, still needing care, when out of the blue Phoebe Fairfax suddenly suggested, 'I wonder, Sabina, if you'd like to come and have a cup of tea with me tomorrow?'

'Yes, well, I—' Sabina broke off, floundering. No way! shrieked her head but, her sensitivities caught, a blunt refusal seemed stuck in her throat. Oh, grief, with Yorke away, not to mention her other grandson being away, poor Mrs Fairfax was housebound, fragile and lonely! Sabina's heartstrings were well and truly pulled. 'I'd love to...' she actually heard herself accept before she had got a grip on herself. *Heavens above!* 'But—' she went on urgently.

'But you don't know the way to Mulberry House,' Mrs Fairfax interrupted her before she could rush on. 'I know Warwickshire may seem a long way, but Yorke assures me it's no distance from London at all. I live in the village of Norvington, and usually use the train myself. But if you...' But while Mulberry House, Norvington, Warwickshire registered and Sabina's thoughts were racing on as to how best to break it to this lovely lady that she would not be making a trip anywhere near the county of Warwickshire tomorrow, she found that Mrs Fairfax, having given her directions, was concluding, 'Now, I know how extremely busy you career women are, so I won't take up any more of your valuable time, but will look forward to seeing you any time after three tomorrow afternoon.' And, with that, she was gone.

'Mrs Fairfax!' Sabina exclaimed anyway, in panicking hope. But the line was dead. Stunned, Sabina stared at the phone in her hand. Had she just accepted...? She hadn't! She couldn't have! Could she? Oh, grief. She knew jolly well that she had!

Sabina was still sitting there trying to get her head together when two minutes later Chris Dawson came into her office. 'About tomorrow,' he began, a determined sort of light in his eye.

'Sorry, Chris, I've made arrangements to visit a sick— friend in Warwickshire tomorrow,' she replied, a date with Chris suddenly seeming much the better of the two options.

'I'll drive you down if you like,' he at once volunteered. That'd be ducky! Such a complication she did not need.

She shook her head. 'My friend has recently had major surgery. She isn't up to a lot of visitors,' she turned down his offer—and discovered that Chris, while not the sort to set her world on fire, was as nice as she'd thought him. For he took it exceedingly well.

'She. You said she,' he grinned. 'Your sick friend's a she.'

'True.'

'Then how about Tuesday?'

What could she do? 'Love to,' she answered—and he went out cheerfully whistling—and she went back to not believing that she had agreed to go and see Yorke's grandmother tomorrow, but knowing full well that she had.

She could not go, of course. No way could she go. Yorke would create blue murder if she did, for one thing. Not that that bothered her—mutiny started to enter her soul once again—it was all his fault anyway. If it hadn't been for him, she would never have met his grandmother. Mutiny started to fade when she thought of his poor frail grandmother sitting there lonely and alone, waiting for her to turn up.

She sighed, searched round for some good excuse to give, some appointment she had forgotten about, but had thought of nothing brilliant when she picked up the phone and dialled Directory Enquiries.

Great—Mrs Fairfax was ex-directory! Now what was she going to do? The obvious thing was to write Yorke's grandmother a note. She had her address, and her letter was bound to get to her by tomorrow.

But—what if it didn't? It most likely would, but it was not unknown, out of sheer cussedness, she was sure, for an important letter to take more than a day to reach its destination.

Visions of the frail lady, her surgery scars not yet healed, struggling to make tea for her caused Sabina to quickly reach for the phone again. This time she rang Yorke's private business line.

As expected, Louise Page took her call. 'I'm sorry to bother you—Sabina Constable here,' Sabina said in a rush. 'I know Yorke's away, but I need his grandmother's telephone number.' She pushed a smile into her voice, hoping to convey that she was used to phoning Phoebe Fairfax. 'You don't happen to have it, do you?' Silence the other end—Sabina feared that things were not going well. 'Being ex-directory is all very well,' she ploughed on chattily, hating herself, hating Yorke Mackinnon—and the fact that he apparently employed the most excellent, give-nothing-away PA, 'but...'

'Perhaps you could get Yorke's mother to pass a message on for you,' Louise Page suggested in her best helpful manner. Great! She stood even less chance of getting Mrs Mackinnon's number. For one thing she didn't know where his mother lived and, of a certainty, Louise Page wasn't going to divulge that piece of information either. Not that she would ring his mother! Heaven help her, life was complicated enough already without bringing Yorke's parents into the equation.

'I don't think I will,' Sabina stated. 'I just wanted a quick word with Mrs Fairfax, that's all.'

'I'm sorry,' the PA apologised, 'but I know how concerned Yorke has been about his grandmother recently. He delayed his trip to Japan until after her operation, and only made arrangements when he was able to see definite signs of improvement.'

In other words, he doesn't want her troubled in any way. Very commendable, Sabina was sure, but it did not help her any. 'Thanks anyway,' Sabina said pleasantly, and rang off.

Now what? Sabina wished that she had never phoned Louise Page. All she'd got for her trouble was the information that Yorke was in Japan and that he didn't want his PA giving out the phone number of any member of his family. Frustrating wasn't in it!

Sabina went home from work that evening still wondering what the devil she could do, how she could get a message through to Mrs Fairfax, and wishing she had taken the notion to ring Yorke's mother a little more seriously. Only then, when Yorke's PA would have gone home from her office too, did it dawn on her that there was a very faint chance that Yorke's parents knew all about their son's phoney engagement anyway.

For all she knew, Yorke could have told them what his cousin had been up to, and the steps he'd had to take in the matter of his grandmother's favourite ring. Perhaps Louise Page would have been more forthcoming with his mother's telephone number. The least she could have done was try. For all Sabina judged Yorke to be a man who kept his own counsel, it could well be that he had confided in his mother about his cousin and that ring. She might well, Sabina saw too late, have been able to contact Mrs Mackinnon and, when certain she knew what was going on, could have discussed her dilemma with her.

Sabina still had no idea what she was going to do when she got up the next morning. Her head ached with worrying about it. She took herself off for a long walk and was crucified throughout with thoughts of Yorke's grandmother, frail but brave, sitting there alone, alone and waiting, waiting for her. Sabina was no nearer to finding a solution when, passing a florist's on her way back, she went in and purchased some flowers.

She walked the rest of the way back to the apartment slowly. She looked down at the flowers in her hand and, even while telling herself not to be stupid, that any visit she made to Mulberry House would be fraught with danger, she somehow knew that she had not bought the flowers for herself.

At half past twelve, Sabina could take it no more, and finally gave in. Even as she told herself that she should not be doing this she showered, donned a smart linen two-piece, then got into her car and headed out of London. She had been through too much self-persecution to do anything else. She was wearing a ring on her engagement finger.

She took the route to Warwickshire trying to deny the logic of her head which told her that this visit was a veritable minefield. Why, she barely knew anything about Yorke—how on earth did she think she was going to combat any questions about him?

Her every instinct was to turn around and to go home. Visions of a lonely, convalescent elderly lady—who'd struggled to make tea—spurred her on. Surely she was not such a poor creature that she couldn't cope with a half-hour visit with Yorke's relative.

And what about him? Oh, grief, she wished she hadn't thought about him. He'd be as mad as blazes when he heard what she'd done. Anger arrived, and Sabina was glad of it. So OK, this wasn't supposed to happen; it had meant to be one meeting and one meeting only. But it had been his bright idea for them to be 'engaged', so what right did he have to go trolling off to Japan, leaving her to cope with any complications that ensued?

That there wouldn't have been any complications if she'd told his grandmother straight away that she could not take tea with her was beside the point. Mrs Fairfax's telephone call had been so entirely unexpected, it had been over before she had been able to gather her scattered wits.

By the time Sabina pulled up on the drive of Mulberry House her anger had gone, and she was left feeling anxious, decidedly nervous, and wishing most definitely that she had the sort of conscience which would have allowed her to stay away.

Mulberry House was an impressive many-roomed Georgian building, and, taking the flowers she had bought with her, Sabina went and rang the bell, hoping that Mrs Fairfax did not have too far to walk to come and let her in.

Then the door opened and she realised she'd had no need to worry about over-tiring Yorke's grandmother because a pleasant woman of about fifty stood there. 'Miss Constable?' she enquired pleasantly.

'Yes,' Sabina answered, slightly tense to know who the woman was and what fresh complication might ensue.

She had no need to fear, she discovered, for, 'I'm Hazel Evans, Mrs Fairfax's housekeeper,' she introduced herself. And, stepping back, she added, 'Mrs Fairfax is in the drawing room.'

Sabina followed the housekeeper along a wide hall, realising that she need not have worried about Yorke's grandmother over-exerting herself in preparing the tea. Mrs Fairfax had staff to do that sort of thing for her.

She still looked very frail, Sabina thought when she went into the drawing room. Phoebe Fairfax was attired in smart afternoon dress and as Hazel Evans went out

Sabina hurried over to the high-backed chair where her
hostess was sitting and, after shaking her hand, gave her
the flowers. 'Why, thank you, they're lovely.' She seemed
genuinely touched.

'How are you, Mrs Fairfax?' Sabina enquired, not
wanting her to exert herself getting up.

'Quite well. But I'll be better when you learn to call
me Pebbie as Yorke does,' she smiled, confiding, 'He
couldn't have been more than three when he heard my
late husband call me Phoebe. Pebbie was the best the
little scamp could manage, and I've been Pebbie ever
since.'

Little scamp—Yorke! Somehow Sabina managed to
hold a pleasant smile—she'd lay odds he had been a
swinish child. 'You have a lovely garden,' she uttered,
searching for some uncomplicated subject—the garden
and lawns were lovely.

'The garden's been a joy to me for many years,'
Phoebe Fairfax smiled and, by pure chance, Sabina
having hit on one of her favourite subjects, as Hazel
wheeled the tea-trolley in and took the flowers to put in
water, they discussed horticulture over the teacups.

Things were going far, far better than Sabina had dared
to hope as she revealed how she had, from a child, been
instructed by their own gardener in the appreciation of
such matters.

'You don't live with your parents now, Sabina?' Mrs
Fairfax enquired.

Sabina saw no reason not to answer. So long as Yorke
didn't come into the conversation she was happy to be
open about anything his grandmother asked her. 'I live
in London now,' she replied, and was about to mention
Natalie, in whose apartment she lived, but decided
against it. Perhaps it was better not to say anything about
Natalie. 'My parents live in Surrey,' she added.

'Yorke's parents live in Surrey!' his grandmother commented, and then smiled. 'But you know that already.'

Oh, help. Perhaps it was time she started to make noises about returning to London. She'd only been here about twenty minutes but... Suddenly a sound outside the drawing room caused her to look over to the door.

The door opened—and she didn't believe it. 'Yorke!' his grandmother exclaimed.

Oh, grief! Sabina inwardly quailed as Yorke came purposefully over to her. He had a smile on his mouth for his grandmother's benefit but, from the look of intense fury in his seething dark eyes, there was no mistaking that he was inwardly boiling to see his 'fiancée' there.

'Sabina!' he exclaimed warmly. She had been unaware she had risen to her feet until, his long length blocking her view of his grandmother for a moment, he caught her by the arms, his head coming nearer. 'My God—you've got a bloody nerve!' he raged in a whispered snarl of sound as his mouth met hers. Sabina's heart began to pound; she felt she could barely breathe. 'I've missed you,' Yorke stated warmly, loud enough for his grandmother to hear.

Like a hole in the head, Sabina judged as he let go of her and went over to greet his grandmother; his 'I've missed you' had been solely for his grandmother's benefit. Feeling stunned, shaken, a kaleidoscope of thoughts flashing through her mind, Sabina sank back down onto her chair—oddly, her only concrete thought just then was that that was the second time he had kissed her.

A few moments later she had pulled herself together to realise that it was not the fact of Yorke kissing her that had made her legs go weak, but the fact of seeing him there at all when she had thought him still in Japan.

And a moment after that, recalling his outraged comment about her nerve, Sabina started to get angry herself. Who the devil did he think he was? For two pins she'd tell his grandmother everything. She had never wanted to enter into this deception anyway!

She glanced across at Yorke's grandmother, frail and still recuperating, and as Mrs Fairfax was just answering Yorke's enquiry about her health with, 'I'm feeling on top of the world,' Sabina knew that she just could not tell her. 'But how wonderful of Sabina to come down and see me when she must have known you were coming home today.'

'Sabina's like that,' Yorke smiled.

Rat! Sabina fumed. 'No wonder you fell in love with her,' his grandmother continued, beaming a smile at Sabina—who could only smile back; and grow angrier than ever at one smiling-mouthed but hard-eyed male.

'Who could help it?' he murmured, and, seated beside his grandmother, added in passing, with an icy look to his fiancée, 'I don't remember giving you my grandmother's address, darling.'

Sabina somehow managed to keep a smile in place, but she'd be damned if she'd answer what she knew was really his question: How the hell did you find out where my grandmother lives?

She opened her mouth fully ready to evade his question—but then found that his grandmother was answering for her. 'I telephoned Sabina at her office—you'd told me where she worked.' See! Sabina controlled the urge to stick out her tongue at him and Mrs Fairfax went on, 'I invited Sabina to have tea with me this afternoon and, when she must have known from your phone calls while you were away that you'd be home today, she agreed to come and didn't say a word.'

'Sabina is full of surprises,' Yorke stated—and a short while later Sabina had another surprise for him.

It happened when his grandmother remarked that her grandson looked tired. 'You've been working too hard.' Or something, Sabina thought sniffily as, brightly, Mrs Fairfax hit on a delightful idea. 'Why don't you both stay to dinner tonight?' she suggested. 'Hazel's been filling up the freezer all week as if we're in for a siege; it won't take her a minute to whip something out and defrost it.'

'I—' Yorke began.

But Phoebe Fairfax was truly warming to the idea, and had just had another one—and cheerfully interrupted to declare, 'I know, why don't you save yourself the drive back and stay the night? You'll be more rested by morning.'

No way! Perhaps her eyes had been showing the confidence she felt that Yorke would turn the notion down flat, Sabina thought later. For, from where she viewed the matter, the sooner he could get her away from his grandmother's home, the better he would like it.

But, to her utter astonishment, a challenging light suddenly entered his eyes, and he did not turn down the invitation. Looking her straight in the eye, he accepted for them both. 'We'd love to, wouldn't we, darling?'

Clearly his answer had, Talk yourself out of that, written all over it. You swine! she silently fumed. So OK, he was furious. Furious to have driven down to Mulberry House and seen her car standing on his grandmother's drive. But surely, having heard Mrs Fairfax say how she had invited her... Anger nipped at Sabina again as it dawned on her that Mr Think-on-his-feet over there thought she should have somehow found some way of turning down his grandmother's invitation without offending her.

'You don't look awfully sure, Sabina?' Mrs Fairfax gently cut into Sabina's mutinous thoughts.

Sabina looked at the sweet, frail and elderly lady who had such a monster for a grandson, and wanted to do anything but hurt her feelings. She slid her glance to where, as icy-eyed as ever, as furious with her as ever, Yorke Mackinnon—who had so uncaringly pushed her into a corner—was sitting there waiting, confident that whichever way she did it she would somehow—wriggle though she might—find a way of turning down this, another of his grandmother's invitations.

Confident, was he? Well, nuts to you, sweetheart, she fumed, and, her glance going quickly back to his grandmother, she smiled. 'Anything Yorke says is fine by me.' And, sparing a smile for him too as she flicked her glance back to him again, she added, 'This is a lovely spot, and I'd really love to stay.' She took her smiling, agreeing glance from him and, addressing Mrs Fairfax again, said, 'If I seemed unsure, it was just that I was thinking that I hadn't come prepared. Though...' Sabina glanced at her watch '...the shops will still be open; if I go now, I can pick up the one or two things I'll need...'

'I'm sure we can fix you up with anything...' Phoebe Fairfax, obviously thrilled that they had agreed to stay, began.

'It won't—' Sabina broke off, giving Yorke the space she was certain he would use to come in and backtrack on his acceptance of his grandmother's invitation. But, to Sabina's horror, shatteringly, he did nothing of the kind. Staggered, she stared at him. Uncompromisingly he looked toughly back—and she was forced to continue, 'Actually, it won't—er—take me long to—nip into town.' She needed some space. Quite desperately she needed some space.

Sorely needing to be on her own, she got to her feet— and weathered the look of displeasure Yorke served her as he too rose from his chair.

'I'll get Hazel to make up your rooms—er—room...'
Mrs Fairfax began, and faltered, clearly trying to be
modern but plainly on ground that was new to her.

'Oh, Yorke and I can make up our own rooms,' Sabina
smiled, inwardly starting to boil. She might have let
herself in for suffering to share the same dinner table as
him—she'd be damned if she'd share the same bed. 'I'll
see to mine when I get back if you don't mind.' She
continued to act as if she hadn't a care in the world.
'Stay and have a chat to your grandmother, darling,' she
instructed Yorke blithely, angry enough with him to want
to punch his head; but, the devil on her back, she went
over to him, stretched up tall and lightly kissed his un-
responsive mouth—and got out of there.

The nearest town was five miles away. She was still
trembling with impotent rage when she got there. The
pig! The swine! The utter beast! How could he do that
to her? How could he when all she'd been trying to do
was help? She hated him! Oh, how she hated him!

That hate consumed her as she sped around the shops,
just managing to complete her purchases—nightdress,
underwear, toothbrush and toiletries—before closing
time. How dared *he* be furious with *her*?

Strangely, though, no matter how outraged she was,
nor no matter how much she hated him, Sabina found
that, just the same, she was heading her car back in the
direction of Norvington and not, as she would by far
have preferred, back to London. It was, she full well
knew, purely for his grandmother's sake that she did so.

She had, she admitted, toyed with the idea of not going
back, and leaving it to Yorke—since he was so very
clever—to think up some good reason to explain her absence. But, as her inbred good manners gave a sudden
surge, Sabina knew that, having accepted Mrs Fairfax's
overnight invitation, she would see it through.

Sabina began to have doubts about that, however, when, about half a mile away from Mulberry House, she saw a sleek black car heading towards her. It came closer and she recognised it as the car that had been parked on the drive at Mulberry House the last time she'd seen it. Yorke's car, in fact. The driver flashed its lights and slowed—clearly he wanted her to stop.

Who the devil *did* he think he was? she fumed, not for the first time. Sabina tilted her chin at a defiant angle—and put her foot down. You started it, you finish it, *darling*, she rebelled angrily. If Yorke Mackinnon thought that he would meet her away from the house and halt her so he could give her a piece of his mind then did he have another think coming!

His face was a picture as, nose in the air, she sailed past. My word, he hadn't sweetened up any in her absence!

Sabina cared not a hoot. She would dine at his grandmother's home because that dear soul wished it. And she would spend the night under her roof too, because the alternative—to explain about Rod and how he had stolen that ring—would be too painful for his grandmother to take. But by no chance was she going to put herself in any position where Yorke Mackinnon could take a verbal pot-shot at her.

A car horn being blasted caused her to take a look in her rear-view mirror. She had company! She pressed her foot down harder on the accelerator but was relieved when the country road proved too narrow for Yorke, lights flashing, horn blaring, to overtake her as he otherwise would certainly have done.

On she sped. Only when Mulberry House was in sight did she slacken her speed. Even so, it was her intention as she started up the drive to swiftly exit from her car and be inside the house before Yorke could leave his.

That idea was immediately shelved, however, when as she careered up the drive, she spotted that there was another car—a smart, expensive car—now occupying a position on the drive.

Not only that but, as Sabina checked her speed, a mature couple who had been inspecting the roses until they had heard her roar through the gates now straightened, and were watching as she, with Yorke's car on her tail, progressed—more sedately—past them.

Oh, heck, now what? was all she had time to wonder before, as she braked, turned off the ignition and got out, Yorke—an angry Yorke—came and stood in front of her.

'What...?' was as far as she got, for he was soon to tell her 'what' in no uncertain way.

'You're a walking disaster!' he snarled for starters.

'What did I do now?' she retaliated before he could go on, riled by the unfairness of that, sparks of giving no quarter flashing in her furious brown eyes.

'It's what you didn't do!' he barked. 'If you'd stopped when you knew I wanted you to I'd have warned you that my parents had turned up.'

His parents! Startled, thunderstruck, disbelieving, she stared at him. No! They couldn't...! Oh, Lord! And then it became obvious—with his talk of 'warned you'—that neither his mother nor his father knew anything at all about their 'engagement'!

Oh, heavens, Sabina thought, her fury suddenly as nothing, this is all I need!

CHAPTER FIVE

'DON'T they know the truth?' Sabina blurted out in a rush anyway as she fought not to panic.

'Come and say hello to my parents,' Yorke said evenly, his fury with her hidden as footsteps crunching over the gravel warned of his mother and father's approach. Plainly they had no idea of what was going on!

Oh, heavens above! Deceiving his grandmother in a good cause was one thing but here she was, 'engaged', staying the night, and now meeting his parents—was there no end to it?

Again Sabina wondered how on earth she had got into this. But there was no time then to do more than accept that, for Natalie's sake, she still had to go through with it, because Yorke was introducing her to a very attractive auburn-haired woman in her early fifties and a still dark-haired, tall man around ten years older than his wife.

'My dear,' Dorothea Mackinnon greeted her warmly. 'How pleased I am to meet you.'

'We were beginning to think that there wasn't a woman good enough for our son to marry. But I can see that there is,' beamed Yorke's father—and Sabina had no need to wonder from where Yorke had inherited his charm.

'H-how—nice to meet you both,' she offered lamely, and had never felt so dreadful her whole life. Then she discovered that her ordeal was not yet over—that there was more to come.

'Imagine my amazement when I rang your grand-mother this morning,' Mrs Mackinnon turned to Yorke to confide, 'and Mother said that your fiancée was going to pay her a visit this afternoon.'

'So that's why you hotfooted it down here?' Yorke teased, exchanging smug masculine glances with his father.

And again Sabina wanted to hit him. Particularly since, as Mrs Mackinnon turned her attention to her, it became obvious that there had been an unspoken question in her remark. And, while Sabina was in no doubt that Yorke's amazement on finding her at Mulberry House had far outreached that of his mother, she felt that she hated him that he was leaving it to her to answer what his mother was really asking.

'You didn't—er—know about Yorke and me?' she questioned in return, not prepared to give him a single Brownie point if he was finding some difficulty in lying to his parent.

'He never tells me anything. Though Mother did say how Yorke's fiancée had visited her in hospital. But she'd been through such a lot, through intense pain, poor darling, and was still in great discomfort. And what with the anaesthetic and everything I thought she was just confused.' She smiled. 'I felt it was better to just humour her.'

'I'll bet she loved that,' Yorke murmured, and his mother gave him an acid-tinged, loving look before, ignoring him completely for his sauce, she turned her attention back to the woman she believed her son would marry.

'Which is why, of course, she stubbornly refused to mention it again. But I can't tell you how delighted we are, Sabina,' she beamed, and, looking for and finding that Sabina was wearing an engagement ring said, 'Oh,

my dear, how kind of you to wear Mother's ring—and
to not think it too old-fashioned.'

'You don't—mind?' Sabina asked stiltedly.

'Mind?' Clearly Mrs Mackinnon was mystified.

'Sabina thought that you might like to have
Grandmother's ring,' Yorke put in smoothly.

'My goodness me, no. I'm thrilled to see you wearing
it,' she stated stoutly, and while Sabina was dying a
thousand deaths at this deception—which had gone on
for long enough but about which she felt powerless to
do anything other than go along with—Dorothea
Mackinnon went on to make her feel even more dreadful
by asking what in normal times would have been a quite
natural question—that question being, 'When are you
going to announce your engagement formally?'

'F-formally?' Sabina stuttered.

'When are you going to let the newspapers...?'

Grief! Her father, not to mention her mother, would
go into immediate heart failure to read any such notice
in an 'engagements' column. 'We can't announce anything yet!' she answered on a burst of panic—and,
looking to Yorke for help, hated him with all her being
when all the help she received from him was a lofty,
arrogant look that more or less said, You got yourself
into this—you get yourself out. I didn't ask you to come
down here and you've got one hell of a nerve anyway.
Fear, panic, hate spurred her on. 'I—er—I'm afraid
my—um—father's being a bit...' She coughed, wished
that the ground would open up and swallow her, but of
course it didn't—and she was forced to go on. 'My
father's being a little—er—sniffy—about it, I'm afraid,'
she managed to get out, and could cheerfully have taken
an antagonistic swipe at one Yorke Mackinnon when he,
not to mention his parents, stared at her in disbelief.

'Sniffy?' his mother queried faintly, as if quite unable to comprehend that someone might doubt the Mackinnon first-class pedigree.

'He'll get used to the idea soon,' Sabina found herself inventing, shrivelling up inside, no end to her perjury. 'It's just that—er—I'm his only child—er—only daughter. He—just needs a little more time to—get used to the idea. So we—Yorke and I—' she included him but was afraid to look at him in case she could not hide the seething inner fury she felt with him '—we thought we wouldn't announce it just yet.'

'Daddy's little girl, eh?' Yorke's father seemed to understand straight away. 'You must come from a very loving home, Sabina.'

'I do,' she smiled, glad that about that, at least, she didn't have to lie.

'Did you manage to get all your shopping done, darling?' Thank you, Yorke, you've been a great help!

'Just,' she answered, flicking him a glance and not thanking him that only now, when she felt as though she'd been pulled through a wringer, had he decided to come to her aid.

'I'll take you up and show you where you'll be sleeping, shall I?' he offered kindly.

Go to blazes, she fumed, but smiled. 'I could do with freshening up.' She looked at his parents, relieved that she would soon be away from them and that the need to add more to her tally of lies would soon be ended— once she got to her room, she was determined she would stay there until they had departed Mulberry House.

She opened her mouth to say her goodbyes—and then felt her spirits sink—her thoughts about Yorke's parents being about to leave were premature, it seemed. 'And, since we're staying to dinner too, I'd better go and give Hazel a hand,' Dorothea Mackinnon commented cheerfully. 'She won't want me to, I know, but . . .'

Oh, God, Sabina thought in despair, and as Mr and Mrs Mackinnon made their way indoors she excused herself and returned to her car for her purchases, her mind in a turmoil.

She ignored Yorke, but he was right there beside her, and together they entered the house.

'Had I better put my head round the drawing-room door and say hello to your grandmother?' She hadn't wanted to say a word to him, but manners were manners, and could not, no matter how against the grain it went, be ignored.

'My grandmother's upstairs resting!' he clipped, and Sabina didn't know how she stopped herself from hitting him. *She* was furious—so what right did he have to sound quietly simmering?

Her feeling that he was quietly steaming was soon borne out when, crossing the hall and climbing the stairs with her, Yorke escorted her to a door at the far end of the long landing. Without a word he opened the door and stood back. She went in. But when she turned, ready to shut the door on him, she discovered that Yorke Mackinnon had no intention of being shut out and that he was inside her bedroom with her—and it was he who closed her bedroom door.

It was, she realised, the first time they had been alone together since he had arrived at Mulberry House and found her there. The first time since he had managed to get in those snarled words on the subject of her nerve. Well, if he thought he was going to carry on from there and go in for some more tongue-lashing, did he have another think coming!

'Do you mind very much leaving—?' was as far as she got.

'Would you mind telling me what in sweet hell you think you're playing at?' he slammed, enraged, through her words, as if she hadn't spoken.

Did she have news for him! 'Don't you come that attitude with me!' she snapped, sorely in need to lash out at him physically but somehow managing to hang onto that last strand of control. 'I didn't want to become *engaged* to you in the first place—'

'In the first place you were only to see my grandmother that one time!' he sliced her off, his dark eyes glinting with fury. 'The only reason I let you anywhere near her orbit was to—'

'You *let* me?' Sabina flared, too incensed at his suggestion that she wasn't good enough to breathe the same air as his grandmother to appreciate the pleasure in cutting him off for a change. 'As I remember it, Mr High-and-Mighty, it was you who had the brilliant idea I go to see her to start with.'

'To start with, you were only meant to see her so you could show her that ring! So she should know that there was one very good reason why I wasn't returning it!' he rapped. And, while some of Sabina's aggression was dented as she remembered how poorly his grandmother had been and the spur his grandmother had needed to regain her fighting spirit, Yorke Mackinnon promptly recharged Sabina's own fighting batteries again by demanding furiously, 'So what the devil do you mean by waiting until my back's turned, until I'm out of the country, and coming down—?'

'Your back's turned!' Sabina shrieked, incensed, aggression back in full force. How *dared* he? 'I didn't even know you *were* out of the country until Mrs Fairfax phoned yesterday afternoon and invited me down to tea.'

'And you couldn't wait to hotfoot it down here and try to endear yourself...'

'Look here, *you*!' Sabina spat, poking a vicious finger at his chest. 'I don't know what type of women you normally mix with—though, from my experience of you, any woman would want her head testing to take you on—

but there's no earthly reason why I should want to endear myself to your grandmother or anyone else!' My stars— she'd kill him! 'The only reason I came down today,' she stormed on, veritable sparks flashing in her eyes, 'was because I'm so unused to the sort of subterfuge which no doubt you dabble in every day, you're so good at it, that I wasn't quick enough to get my thoughts together and invent some excuse for not coming. And since Mrs Fairfax had rung off before I had got my thoughts together to tell her I couldn't make it, I couldn't see what else to do. I tried ringing your PA, but she wouldn't give me your grandmother's phone number, so what could I do? Mrs Fairfax sounded lonely and—'

'Lonely!' he erupted. 'She's half the village popping by to see her. There's always someone here when—'

'*I* didn't know that, did I? All I knew was that you were away—Lord knew for how long. Rod Lacey's away too, and I didn't know what the situation was with your parents. So she could—'

'Huh!' he grunted, and she came the closest yet to hitting him.

'Huh to you too, Mackinnon,' she hurled at him hotly. 'And believe what the hell you like. My only reason for being here today is the one I've stated.'

'Because my PA wouldn't give you my grandmother's number and you couldn't bear to think of her being lonely?' he questioned sceptically—or was there an edge of something else in his voice? He certainly didn't seem as angry as he had been.

Sabina didn't give a button whether he was angry or not. 'That's about it,' she answered stiffly. 'I kept getting a picture of a frail, lonely lady, having struggled to make tea—I didn't know her circumstances—that she had a housekeeper—so how could I leave her sitting there, lonely, waiting? I didn't want to come,' she added woodenly, and, looking at him, noticed that there seemed to be a hint of softening in the dark depths of his eyes. Oddly, she found that softening, when he had been so furious, more disturbing than his anger. 'I—er—I—um—was afraid to trust the post in case any letter I wrote didn't...'

'You—worried about her?' Yorke questioned evenly, nothing at all harsh about his tone now.

It had a peculiar effect on Sabina. She felt weakened. But, knowing what a sharp and to-the-point monster he could be, she most definitely did not want to be weakened.

That being so, aggressiveness seemed to be the only antidote to any such weakness. 'This has gone far enough!' she decided. Oh, dear—the slight narrowing of his eyes told her he did not like her sharper attitude. Well, tough—here was some more of the same. 'You'd better go and tell everyone that we're not engaged after all,' she told him loftily.

Any softening she had imagined in him disappeared entirely at her tone. Clearly he had no liking for bossy women. Flint glinted in his eyes as he silently studied her. And his tone was curt and to the point when a moment later he countered, 'I will—when you've given me back that ring.'

'Damn you!' she spat. And again it was impasse. But, frustrating though it was to have to stand there and take it, somehow, and from somewhere, Sabina found control—and with it an idea. Since she wasn't getting anywhere by firing up to him, might she not have the satisfaction of making him squirm if he thought it mattered not a whit to her? So she smiled. He held her glance. She knew he was wary. Wary and waiting. 'Do you know, Yorke,' she smiled, after keeping him waiting only another second longer, 'I do believe I shall quite enjoy being engaged to you.'

It was she who waited this time—for his reaction. Because for all of two seconds he just stood and stared at her, his glance taking in her impudent expression. Then, with not a squirm in sight, nor yet another of his short and sharp insults aimed her way, Yorke leaned back fractionally—and grinned. He actually grinned. And she was weakened. Despite herself, that grin weakened her.

And, she owned, she was having a hard time getting her head together, when casually, that grin becoming a smirk, he queried, 'Even though my family aren't good enough for yours?'

'Good en—? Ah!' Light dawned. All too plainly he was referring to her evasive comment to his parents about her father being a little 'sniffy' about their 'engagement'.

'Cheeky baggage!' he becalled her amiably—and, strangely, she just had to laugh.

'Nothing personal,' she replied, her mouth turning upwards. Then she became aware of Yorke's intent look on her mouth and, for no reason that she could think of, as he stared as if fascinated so her heart fluttered crazily. 'Anyhow,' she began hurriedly, 'that was no worse than you intimating some minutes ago that I wasn't good enough to breathe the same air as your grandmother.'

'Ah!' It was his turn to remember. 'Are you going to forgive me for being just a touch over-protective of a quite remarkable lady who's been so seriously ill and who means a lot to me?' he asked coaxingly.

My heavens—that charm! Sabina felt her legs go weak. What could she do? She smiled. 'I don't see why not,' she conceded, any offence she had taken dead and buried.

Again she was aware of his glance on her smiling mouth. He moved forward—and she instinctively knew that he was going to kiss her. Just as she knew that he was giving her all the time in the world to move away.

But she did not move away. Could not move away. She seemed somehow mesmerised by him. He was close up to her now, his hands on her arms, and suddenly she was no longer smiling—and nor was he.

It was meant to be a quiet, brief kiss. She somehow knew that. Just a light touching of mouths. A sort of mutual 'I'm sorry for any offence caused or taken' kind of kiss. And perhaps it did start out that way. For Sabina felt his mouth on hers in a light touch—at first. Then, with his superb mouth over hers, and as her heart started to race, she felt his strong, manly arms come about her. Felt herself being pulled—unresisting, it had to be said— closer up to him. Lingeringly he kissed her, and without being fully aware of it she held onto him.

When he broke that kiss, Sabina didn't know quite where she was. She stared up into his warm dark eyes, vaguely aware of her own warm colour as Yorke looked into her upturned face. Then suddenly he was putting her abruptly away from him—and she was alone.

Sabina stared at the door after he had gone. Good heavens! She felt totally stunned at what he could do to her. How, without even trying, he could make her feel. She had been—enthralled! Not threatened, or alarmed, and—for one who was, as Yorke himself had suggested might be the case, choosy—certainly not one tiny bit affronted—just enthralled.

He had kissed her before—for his grandmother's benefit. But that kiss just now, given and received, not to mention returned, had been personal, between just Yorke and her. Oh, grief!

Sabina turned from the door. For goodness' sake, it had been a mere kiss, nothing more. Think about something else, do. She wandered over to the bed, realised that the bed had been made, that in her absence at the shops Hazel had been up and, despite her saying that she would do it, had made her room ready.

That thought about shops triggered off the memory
of the items she had purchased. She had no recollection
of dropping them down on the chest of drawers, but
that was where her packages were.

She went to retrieve them, then heard a sound coming
from the next-door room and turned and stared at the
dividing wall. It was Yorke's room; she knew it. What
was more natural than that Mrs Fairfax should give her
a room where she would feel comfortable and where she
would feel secure—next to the man she 'loved'?

Only then did Sabina take time to glance about her.
There were two other doors in the room apart from the
one that led out to that elegant landing. In one there
was a key in the keyhole, but not in the other.

She investigated the other room first. It was a
bathroom, with everything she might possibly need in
there, including a Cellophane-wrapped new toothbrush
and a freshly laundered if very oversized white towelling
robe.

Sabina returned to the bedroom, her eyes now riveted
to the key in the door which just had to be a communicating door to Yorke's room.

She listened, but could hear no sound now. But, even
so, it was too soon after that kiss for her to want to see
Yorke again. Which she might well do if she went over
and turned the handle to check if it was locked. She
needed more time before she saw him again. Though
why she needed more time she had no clue. She had
been kissed before, for pity's sake—and, she owned, with
a degree more passion. So why had Yorke's unde-
manding—if lingering—kiss disturbed her so?

Oh, hang it! she fumed, suddenly cross with herself
that the embrace she had shared with Yorke seemed to
be stuck solid to the forefront of her mind. Irritated with
herself, she went quickly over to the communicating
door. And there her movements slowed.

Hardly daring to breathe for fear of making a sound that might be heard by the next-door occupant, she stretched out a hand to the key, grasped it, and silently endeavoured to turn it to the right. It did not budge. The door was already locked.

Good! Sabina came away from the door and with Yorke's grandmother resting and his mother helping Hazel, and Yorke himself next door—for all she could no longer hear him—she decided that there was no need for her to hurry from her room either. She went and had a bath.

Nor was she in any hurry to join any of the family when, dressed once more in her linen two-piece, her night-black hair brushed and shining to her shoulders, she checked her appearance. Somehow, while before that kiss she'd no problem that she would have to wear the same outfit for dinner that she had worn all afternoon, now it seemed a touch not right after all. Oh, bother that kiss!

Sabina forced her mind away from something which she was certain Yorke had not given another second's thought to, and concentrated instead on the evening before her that had, somehow, to be got through.

She guessed that because Mrs Fairfax was still recuperating she would go to bed early, and therefore dine more early than she would normally. But, with not only Yorke's grandmother there at the dinner table but his parents too, Sabina was not keen to spend more time in their company—when who knew what lies she would have to tell—than she had to.

Bitterly then did she regret that 'I'd really love to stay' with which she had accepted Mrs Fairfax's invitation. It was all down to Yorke, of course. He should never have goaded her into it. Or perhaps she should never have let him, or his confidence that she would refuse the invitation, goad her into accepting it.

Memory of his kiss tried to intrude, but this time in dismissing it Sabina realised that Yorke would be there this evening too. And that since it was his grandmother they were guarding—the shock of discovering that Rod Lacey had stolen her favourite ring and had given it to his girlfriend was something she must never experience either in this stage of her recovery—then for certain Yorke would take every care that his grandmother learned nothing at all about it.

That went for his parents too—though... Suddenly she could see no earthly reason why Yorke's parents should not know. Sabina was in complete agreement that for the sake of Mrs Fairfax's health she would have to go along with the 'engagement', but could see no possible reason why Yorke's parents should not be told the truth.

A sound in the adjoining room disturbed her. She glanced at her watch. It was five to seven. She heard a door nearby close. Then, as she stood still and listened, someone came and tapped lightly on her door. She knew it was Yorke.

She felt butterflies in her stomach at just the thought of seeing him again. Oh, for goodness' sake, she thought impatiently. Just because the man had held her in his arms!

That impatience carried her to the door. 'Oh, hello,' she offered casually on seeing Yorke, tall, dark-haired and definitely handsome, standing there.

'Hello, yourself,' he answered, his casual tone beating hers into a cocked hat. 'Dinner's in a few minutes. Are you ready?'

'As I'll ever be,' she replied, in case he thought she was looking forward to this.

'You'll be all right,' he assured her as she came from her room.

She was glad he thought so, but they had gone along the landing and had started down the stairs before she got her head sufficiently together to suddenly announce, 'Look, I know, and I suppose I accept, in the interests of your grandmother's improving health, that I have to go along with this.'

'There is an alternative,' Yorke murmured... and Sabina felt a swift return of her ear-boxing tendencies. No way was she going to give him that ring. It wasn't hers to give.

'But,' she went doggedly on, 'I can't think of one single, solitary reason why we can't tell your parents the truth.'

They had reached the bottom of the elegant staircase, but there Sabina halted, stubbornly refusing to move another step. Any minute now they would be joining his family. She wanted this settled. Surely he would be able to get his parents alone to explain the situation to them!

'You can't?' Yorke halted too, his glance raking her suddenly mutinous expression.

'No, I can't!' she retorted, ignoring the idiotic flutter in her heart region as her eyes met his. She looked from his eyes down to his mouth, his wonderful mouth that had kissed hers. 'No, I can't!' she repeated, jerking herself hastily away from such nonsensical thoughts. Great heavens—what *was* the matter with her?

'You can't see that my mother, by omission if nothing else, would have to lie to *her* mother?'

Sabina dragged her thoughts back to the subject under discussion. Damn him to hell! She knew that she would find it extremely difficult, not to say impossible to lie to her own mother, so, devil take it, she could hardly force an issue which would mean his mother lying to hers.

'You've lied to yours!' she reminded him pithily.

'It was rather thrust upon me...' *he* reminded *her* equably, adding, 'Better me than her.'

There was no answer to that. 'Do you always have to be so aggravatingly protective of the women you care for?' she snapped.

'Always!' he answered, and, looking down at her, he breathed in an undertone, 'Smile—here come my parents.'

By the time they had exchanged greetings with his parents Sabina had started to recover from the oddest of all notions—that she would not mind being protected by him. Rot! What utter rot! That implied that she wanted him to care for her a little, too, didn't it? Oh, for goodness' sake!

'Mother's waiting for us in the dining room,' Dorothea Mackinnon smiled at Sabina, and, taking her arm in friendly fashion, she steered her in a direction Sabina had not yet visited.

In no time they were all seated, Sabina placed in between Yorke and his grandmother, with Mr and Mrs Mackinnon seated on the other side of the table.

Talk was general for a while as they tucked into a most delicious cold cucumber soup. But the general conversation was not to last. And Sabina, who had begun to think that if the remainder of the meal continued like this then she might even begin to enjoy it, grew immediately tense when, with poached salmon, new potatoes, peas and a side salad before her, Yorke's mother stated warmly, 'I can't tell you how delighted we are to meet you, Sabina.' And while Sabina was still searching for some kind of an answer she was going on, equally warmly, 'How long have you and Yorke known each other?'

'Um . . .' Sabina hesitated, hoping to convey that she was calculating from the time she had first met Yorke. But she desperately needed help. To say a little over two weeks would have his intelligent grandmother putting more than two and two together. Suddenly, though, even while in a panic trying to think up an answer, Sabina started to get annoyed with Yorke. For heaven's sake, it was as much his problem as hers! She looked from his mother to him, her colour a tinge pink from her burst of crossness with him. 'How long is it, Yorke?' she asked nicely.

His dark gaze travelled her face, and, clearly having observed her emotional colour, his mouth quirked up at the corners. 'Long enough, wouldn't you say, darling?' he murmured.

Too long, she silently fumed—damn him, she hadn't missed the barb behind his 'Long enough'. But Mrs Mackinnon, after an affectionate glance to her son, was going on to enquire happily, 'Where did you and Yorke meet?'

It was a natural question, she realised. One which any pleased and interested future mother-in-law might ask. 'We met...' she began, and then found that, as she could not lie to her own mother, neither could she lie to Yorke's mother. She did the only thing possible—she again turned and looked at Yorke. And to her surprise he at once smiled—a comforting 'don't worry' kind of smile— and she could only wonder that he must have read the distress signals flying in her eyes.

Then, while the rhythm of her heart seemed momentarily haphazard for no particular reason, she discovered that she did not have to lie to his mother. And that nor would Yorke verbally lie to his mother, when he smiled, 'It's no secret, darling,' and, taking his glance from her, he took on his parent's question and answered, 'We met through Rod, actually.'

'Rodney!' his grandmother exclaimed, and, looking at Sabina, asked, 'You know my other grandson?'

'Rod dated my girlfriend,' Sabina stated truthfully.

'Ah!' Phoebe Fairfax beamed.

And that, it seemed, was all the explanation that was needed as the conversation drifted on to Rodney Lacey—who was clearly loved by both his grandmother and his aunt—and how they'd heard he had given up his job—an everyday occurrence, apparently—and how he had been a little tardy in his communication just lately.

'It wouldn't hurt him to pick up the phone and enquire how you are,' Dorothea Mackinnon opined to her mother.

'I'd begin to think my surgery wasn't so one hundred per cent successful as Yorke assures me it was if he did!' Phoebe Fairfax commented drily. And her daughter laughed—and then turned her attention back to Sabina.

'You didn't meet Yorke through your work, then,' she stated pleasantly, and thought to tack on, 'You *do* work, though?'

'Dorothea!' Emmet Mackinnon muttered quietly.

His wife looked a tinge discomfited, and it was a shade apologetically that she went on, 'Forgive me, my dear, but, even though Emmet has said I mustn't ask questions of you, you are the girl our son is going to marry, so it's only natural that...'

'Of course it is.' Sabina could only help her out. Even while wanting only to stay quiet throughout the remainder of the meal—and let Yorke do all the talking for her—she just had to step in and help Mrs Mackinnon over any embarrassment she was enduring. 'I work for a computer company.'

'You work with computers?'

'Mainly secretarial,' Sabina confessed, and added, 'I enjoy it.'

'Will you want to carry on with your work after you and Yorke are married?' Grief! 'So many young women do nowadays,' Mrs Mackinnon commented—as if to show that she understood.

'We haven't really discussed it, have we?' Sabina turned to Yorke for help.

'I think it will be a full-time job looking after me,' Yorke drawled teasingly, and, while Sabina was of the opinion that he was big enough to look after himself, he grinned that devastating grin that made her legs go weak—and Sabina looked hastily away from him.

And, while he went on to engage his father in some engineering topic to do with his father's latest car, she gave herself a stern lecture on not being so ridiculous and the fact that nobody's grin was so devastating that it could make anyone's legs go weak. And, for goodness' sake, the pudding stage having been reached, dinner would soon end, and Yorke's parents would go home, then his grandmother would go to bed and so would she—and never, never, ever again, she vowed, would she repeat this experience.

'I know you said that your parents are a wee bit unhappy about losing you—' Mrs Mackinnon broke into her thoughts '—but if there's anything we can do to reassure them—'

'It will sort itself out, Mother,' Yorke cut in quietly.

'Yes, of course. Of course it will,' she agreed. 'It's just that your father and I—' Mrs Mackinnon broke off as her husband glanced at her when she started taking his name in vain. 'Well, anyway—' she opted to go up another avenue '—I'm sure that Yorke has already been able to part persuade your father that he'll—' Again she broke off, but this time clearly because of what she read in Sabina's unguarded expression. 'You have...?' Swiftly she turned her attention to her son. 'Haven't you met Sabina's parents?' she asked—and Sabina knew from where Yorke got some of his straight talking. 'Surely you've asked Sabina's father for— ?'

'Perhaps they don't do things like that these days,' Phoebe Fairfax butted in, plainly ready to take up

cudgels should anyone attempt to have a go at her be-
loved grandson—her daughter included.

'I would hope Yorke has been brought up better than
to not know...'

Oh, heavens. Sabina took her glance away from
Yorke's mother and turned to see that Yorke seemed not
the slightest put out that his mother appeared to be taking
him to task over his lack of manners.

Her eyes met his. He smiled, her heart fluttered, and
she glanced quickly away, her look connecting with the
steady gaze of his father, who, after silence had reigned
for a moment, commented, 'I hear your family hail from
Surrey too, Sabina,' his comment so easing any small
strain in the atmosphere that she smiled at him grate-
fully, and answered quite without thinking.

'My father has a component factory there, in—' Oh,
heavens. She broke off, fearing she had revealed too
much.

And had, she was at once aware when, even as she
drew fresh breath, Yorke's father was exclaiming, 'Not
Constable Components!'

'That's—us,' she had to confirm on a panicky gulp
of breath.

'But—I know your father!' Emmet Mackinnon declared. 'We belong to the same golf club!' And Sabina
went into shock. 'Why didn't you say, Yorke?' His father
turned his attention to his son, which caused Sabina to
realise that Yorke must have heard of her father's
company too—though not of her connection with it—
and subsequently how she came from a monied back-
ground. Well, sucks boo to him; he shouldn't have made
it sound as if he thought she had her eye to the main
chance when he'd turned up today and found her there.

'The situation is a degree or two delicate,' Yorke informed his father. Delicate! It was positively fragile—
about to fracture at any minute. She'd felt as if she had

been treading on eggs before, but now . . . Oh, where was her bed?

'Because of Mr Constable's attitude to Sabina getting engaged?' Dorothea Mackinnon came in, and then a sudden, wonderful idea striking her, she suggested, 'Perhaps Emmet and I should invite your parents to dinner one evening, Sabina. Your father already knows Yorke's father. But it might allay any fears your mother might have if we spent an evening together and talked through any small worry.'

Oh, my God! 'Er. . .' Sabina choked helplessly.

'I'd like both your parents to know that, as well as Yorke keeping you safe, you'll be safe in our family, that you'll be regarded as one of our own.'

It had to stop! And stop now! Sabina was racked with guilt and could not take it. Had she truly been engaged to Yorke then she would have considered his mother's comments most loving and welcoming. But she was not engaged to him. It was all a sham. These people were nothing to her and she, a non-liar, was getting enmeshed deeper and deeper into this lie. And, what was worse, if she did not take steps to stop it now, then her mother and father were going to be involved—and she couldn't have that.

Dorothea Mackinnon was waiting for a reply. Sabina took a deep breath and, grabbing hold of all the courage she could muster, she was ready. Unfortunately, as she opened her mouth to state something along the lines of, Look, I'm not engaged to your son. Yorke and I are not planning to marry, she happened to glance at Phoebe Fairfax.

Oh, Lord. Even as she hurriedly took her glance away from the frail elderly lady so Sabina's resolve folded. How could she say anything, confess anything? She had witnessed for herself that Mrs Fairfax loved her grandson Rod Lacey, and, despite the fact that she was making

good progress in her recovery, she still wasn't up to
hearing of his wickedness in stealing one of her favourite
possessions.

'I . . .' she said helplessly, her glance going down to her
left hand and that ring on her engagement finger—only
to feel a quite violent reaction when all at once she saw,
felt, Yorke's right hand come and take a hold of that
hand.

Her glance shot to his and she stared, startled, at him,
oblivious for the moment of anyone else in the room.
She had no idea what she had expected to see in the dark
depths of his eyes—perhaps irritation with her if he had
read anything of her thoughts and suspected that now,
at the eleventh hour, so to speak, after having weathered
the whole of the mealtime, she was about to blow everything. But, as she continued to stare at him, Sabina could
glimpse no sign of irritation or annoyance. Just—
gentleness, and understanding!

She could hardly believe it. She had known him tough,
hard-hitting—and yet here he was—gentle! She felt pink
warm her cheeks when staggeringly, in the next
moment—in a moment of pure empathy, as if he knew
all about her troubled conscience—Yorke raised her hand
to his lips and kissed the back of it.

Her heart started to pound, and as she looked at him
and he looked back at her it seemed as if no one else
existed.

But they did exist. Some small sound in the room
caused her to look from him to his mother, who was
looking a little misty-eyed, then to his grandmother, who
was looking much the same.

She pulled her hand from his tight hold and had never
felt so confused in her life when, letting go of her hand,
Yorke commented generally, self-deprecatingly, 'You
know how it is,' as if to explain his moment of ten-
derness with her. And, even though that too—that hint

that they cared for each other—was a lie, Sabina felt so shaken that she just had to go along with it. Then Yorke was suggesting to his mother, 'Perhaps we'll keep the congratulatory dinner on hold for the moment.' And, turning to his grandmother, he added, 'I'm sure your physician wouldn't approve of you being up so late, Pebbie.'

'It's barely nine o'clock,' she reprimanded him sharply. 'But,' she added with a smile, 'it's been such a marvellous day. Perhaps I shouldn't ruin it by getting over-tired.'

'I'll come up with you,' her daughter declared at once, and after Mrs Fairfax had left the room and Dorothea Mackinnon had gone with her to help her into bed Sabina was left with Yorke and his father.

Quite desperately then did she want to implore Emmet Mackinnon not to breathe a word to her father if they should bump into each other at the golf club, but she was still so utterly confused by Yorke's simple act of kissing her hand that she found it totally impossible to find a tactful way of doing it.

Then Dorothea Mackinnon was rejoining them and Yorke's father was commenting that if they wanted to get back to Surrey before midnight they had better leave now, and then she and Yorke were going with them out to the drive to see them off.

'Goodbye, Sabina. Today has been a real thrill for me,' Yorke's mother smiled, and to add yet more guilt to the heap Sabina was nursing she caught hold of her impulsively and kissed her cheek.

'Welcome to the family, my dear,' Emmet Mackinnon said warmly, and he too kissed her.

And Sabina just couldn't take any more. No sooner had he started the car and begun steering down the drive than she turned about and went indoors. She was confused, mixed up, awash with guilt, and felt she did not want to say another word to Yorke that night.

He, it seemed, had nothing he wanted to say to her either. For he made no attempt to detain her, and she went quickly across the hall to the stairs. No doubt Yorke would spend some minutes downstairs securing the house for the night.

Sabina had been in her room some ten minutes when she heard the door to the room next door open and close. Oh, heavens, what the dickens was the matter with her? She hated him, didn't hate him.

But what about that gentleness, that empathy? Had she imagined it? And what about this evening's complications—the complication of Yorke's father knowing her father? Oh, Lord! It just didn't bear thinking about! Confusion! Everything was just one huge, complete, mixed-up mess.

CHAPTER SIX

SABINA reckoned that she counted every hour of that long night, and at four on Sunday morning she knew she'd had enough of trying to sleep.

It was midsummer and therefore already getting light when she left her bed and went and sat in a chair, the worries of that endless night still plaguing her. Though it was no wonder to her that she could not sleep—not with all the heavy guilt she had on her conscience.

How she ever could have assisted Yorke in deceiving his parents the way she had she could not now believe. She had liked them, for goodness' sake!

Yet, on thinking about it, how could she not have aided that deception when the alternative would have and could still, trigger off more heart trouble for Mrs Fairfax? Or at the very least sap some of her will to recover.

She had looked a little stronger than she had in hospital, though, Sabina reflected. Perhaps if Yorke did break the news to her, very gently... Sabina's thoughts faltered as she recalled on the instant the gentleness, the understanding she had read in his eyes. Her thoughts wavered some more as she went on to relive that moment when he had raised her hand to his lips and kissed it.

Quite unconsciously, Sabina raised her left hand to her face and rubbed the back of it against her cheek. A moment later she realised what she was doing, muttered crossly, 'Oh, for goodness' sake!' and went back to her thoughts that perhaps Yorke might, sensitively, be able to now tell his grandmother about Rod Lacey's dis-

honesty. Maybe Yorke could also tell her about Natalie—
and why she, Sabina, could not let her have her ring
back yet.

Then she remembered how fragile Mrs Fairfax still
looked, and she sighed. The poor dear, she had been
through enough of a traumatic time of it as it was. It
would be cruel, not to say heartless to tell her of Rod's
perfidy.

With a great deal of reluctance, Sabina realised that
there was nothing for it but that she would have to go
along with Yorke on this one. Particularly since, on
thinking back, this whole business had only started because Yorke had given his grandmother his word that
he would return her ring only when he was certain she
was going to pull through that trauma.

At that point Sabina's thoughts started to grow confused again. Oh, what a mess! But, if she accepted that,
conceded that, yes, it had to be right to deceive Yorke's
grandmother, then no way was she going to let a word
of this get back to her own parents. No way was she
going to deceive them.

Sabina tried to quieten a sudden flutter of panic that
everything seemed to be getting away from her. Once
she left Mulberry House today, she reminded herself,
she personally would have no need to deceive anyone.
She would take jolly good care, should Mrs Fairfax ring
her again and invite her to tea, that she had some good
excuse ready for not accepting.

But she started to panic again, as she had again and
again in the night, at the thought of Yorke's father and
her father bumping into each other on the golf course.
Oh, heavens! Worse, what if Yorke's mother, regardless
of her son's 'Perhaps we'll keep the congratulatory dinner
on hold for the moment', took it into her head to phone
her mother to comment on how pleased she was that her
son was to marry her daughter?

Ye gods! It didn't bear thinking about. Sabina was unable to sit still at that thought and shot off her chair to begin pacing up and down. Yorke hadn't asked his mother not to contact her mother, had he? Nor had he suggested that his father should not say a word to hers.

Oh, crumbs! Her parents were so protective of her, they'd be on the phone or calling at her address post-haste at the merest mention that she was involved with someone.

Suddenly Sabina was a mass of agitation at the thought that, while it was a certainty that she could not lie to them, at the same time she considered it would be a distinct disloyalty to Natalie to tell her parents the truth—that Natalie's fiancé was a thief.

Sabina was still abstractedly pacing up and down when she all at once became aware of how frequently her glance was darting to the communicating door that separated her room from the one next door.

All Yorke wanted was for her to hand over that ring. But, even while she knew that by handing over that ring she could end it all, she could not do it. How could she? It would mean letting Natalie down—and she just couldn't do it.

She could just imagine the conversation when Natalie returned: 'Where's my ring?' 'I gave it to Rod's cousin.' 'Why?' 'Because Rod, the man you're in love with, stole it.' Oh, hell, the whole thing was a nightmare!

Her glance fastened on that connecting door again—and suddenly Sabina was up in arms. She went and took a look at her watch. Five o'clock and daylight and—dammit—why should he peacefully sleep when she was fast growing a demented wreck at the horrifying thought of her parents and his parents communicating?

With all Yorke Mackinnon had on his conscience he should be as guilt-raddled as she. It wasn't fair, and she wasn't having it!

Having agitatedly built herself up into a fine rage, Sabina wanted immediate action. She wasn't feeling very civil, so had no time for civilities. Nor time to shower and dress and to politely wait until she saw him at breakfast.

Working on a full head of steam, Sabina charged full pelt into the bathroom and grabbed up the over-large towelling robe, and in the next few seconds she had inserted her arms and, the garment reaching her ankles and flapping over the ends of her fingers, wrapped it round herself and tied the belt.

And seconds later, still in high dudgeon—if Yorke was asleep then it was about time he woke up—Sabina went charging to the connecting door. It was more than high time, in her opinion, that she got this sorted out.

Without a thought in her head that it might be the housekeeper who was occupying the room for all she knew, Sabina turned the key in the lock while at the same time she pushed open the door.

Considering she had never been in a man's bedroom before—save the room her father shared with her mother—there was a singular lack of bashfulness about her as Sabina stormed into the room, her angry glance focused on the large double bed.

As she had surmised, it was not the housekeeper who occupied it but Yorke Mackinnon. He, like her, slept with the curtains open. But it was only then, as she stared at his sleeping figure, dark-haired, unshaven, relaxed—obviously warm since his only covering was a cotton sheet, the rest of the covers in a heap on the floor—that some realisation of what she was doing struck Sabina. And, while she could not help thinking that even relaxed in sleep his mouth was firm, his face good-looking, she tried hard not to notice the scarcity of his attire. For he had one foot outside the sheet and most of his top half was exposed. She stared fascinated at his manly chest with its central column of dark hair spreading out to his nipples.

Then brought herself up sharply. Only then, as she quickly averted her gaze, did Sabina pause to wonder what was happening to her. She wasn't impulsive; she just was not by nature impulsive. She was cautious, always had been—so what the dickens had this man let loose in her? What was she doing here?

A moment later, however, and her head was clearing. For goodness' sake, she knew why she was here! This had got to be cleared up here and now. Yorke had to be told to make sure his father didn't talk to her father. That his mother didn't...

She glanced at his face—and went hot all over. Yorke had one eye open and was watching her! She supposed she was a rather unexpected, not to say quaint sight, standing there in that all-enveloping robe at just after five in the morning.

That 'quaint' thought made her angry again. It was the push she needed to march up to the bed and look down on him. 'Wake up!' she ordered in no uncertain fashion.

Casually, he opened his other eye, and languidly sat up, and Sabina realised that the heavy thumping of her heart stemmed solely from the unusualness of the situation for her, and not from the fact that Yorke's only covering fell down to his waist—exposing yet more of him to her view.

Somehow then she felt too tongue-tied to say another word. Not that he seemed in any hurry to make conversation either, but seemed content to rest his unhurried gaze on her tousled hair. Most peculiarly, she found she was wishing that she had taken time out to tidy it before she had rushed in here. Oh, grief—she must be going crazy. She opened her mouth, and was there ready with her demands—but found that he was there first.

'I presume the house isn't on fire,' he drawled laconically.

She wanted—needed—her fury, her anger, her outrage back. But, frustratingly, all had deserted her. 'I want to talk to you!' she informed him stiffly, and could have thumped him when, not in the slightest fazed, he stretched out one long bare arm to the table by his bed and checked the time on his watch.

'Did you sleep at all?' he enquired mockingly.

And anger did arrive and she was glad of it. 'This is serious!' she snapped shortly.

Silently Yorke surveyed her. She had an idea that nothing was lost on him—the fact that she was short and snappy and more than a hint anxious. 'The floor's all yours,' he invited, and, moving his legs over a little, he further invited, 'Take a seat and tell me about it.'

There had been few occasions when Sabina had been up at five in the morning—childhood ailments, perhaps, or catching an early holiday flight with her parents, maybe—but never had she imagined that on one Sunday morning at this hour she would be closeted with a male of the species—one she hardly knew and one whom she was growing more and more certain was stark naked beneath that sheet.

'I . . .' she began, about to tell him, I won't sit down if you don't mind. But as that one word left her so she glanced at him, cool, tough and even without a stitch of clothing on managing to convey an air of suave sophistication. And suddenly it seemed a point of honour that he should not think her incredibly naïve. 'Why not?' she shrugged, throwing the return of her natural caution to the winds.

'You're blushing,' Yorke commented idly as she perched herself on the edge of his bed.

She could have crowned him! She had been trying to seem as sophisticated as he—that blush had ruined it all. 'It's the light,' she discounted loftily, and went on in the same lofty vein, 'I'm afraid I'm going to have to insist that you tell your parents the truth about us.'

His expression stilled. Wordlessly he stared at her—and Sabina knew then, if she had not known before, that people just didn't go around telling Yorke Mackinnon what to do and expecting him to do it.

And she was right; that was made plain a few seconds later when Yorke, quite nicely, enquired, 'Now why would I do that?'

'You know why!' she exclaimed crossly. 'I'd no idea that your father knew my father...'

'If you'd mentioned who your father was beforehand, I...'

'I might have mentioned my connections had you not dubbed me some sort of humble secretary without a penny...'

'You? Humble?' he scoffed, and Sabina stared at him. Surely he didn't see her as being as arrogant as she saw him!

'Well...' she mumbled, but swiftly got herself together again to state, 'We're getting off the point.'

'Which is?'

Damn his eyes. He was being deliberately obtuse. 'Your grandmother thinks you're a little scamp!' she threw at him, apropos of nothing but hoping to bruise him a little.

It didn't so much as make him wince. 'And what do you think?' he enquired, his mouth actually daring to pick up at the corners.

'The word "bastard" springs to mind!' she hissed. 'Only nicely brought up girls don't use language like that.'

His answer was to laugh, and even as she at that moment hated him she was at the same time fascinated by his even teeth, his wonderful mouth. As his laughter fell away, though, he looked steadily into her eyes and stated quietly, 'I suspect, Sabina, that you've been extremely nicely brought up.'

What was he saying? Could she take that as a compliment? She coughed a little, wondered if it was the many folds of her towelling covering that made her suddenly feel so warm, and hurriedly broke into speech to advise, 'That's just the point! I was brought up in a very—protected fashion. That protection extending so that, at the merest whisper that I'm involved with someone, my parents will be in touch, needing to know all about it. I can't,' she rushed on, 'I just can't lie to them!' She slowed down and added, 'But nor can I tell them the truth and let Natalie down.'

Yorke stared at her, and she'd have given anything to know what he was thinking. Though she guessed it was something along the lines of, Hand over that ring and you won't have a problem. For he would then tell his parents that they were no longer engaged, and his parents would be far too tactful and well-mannered to say a word to her parents on the subject. It would then be guaranteed that should his father ever be in conversation with her father, then he would discuss every other subject under the sun—apart from his son's brief engagement.

But while she looked back at Yorke, fully expecting him to use the 'return the ring' line, he said nothing of the sort but, to her astonishment, enquired, 'Do I take it from that that you're not involved with anyone at the moment?'

Her mouth fell slightly agape. Good heavens, he was quick! But she had never forgotten his insinuation, given with the rider that she was choosy, that she was a girl who stayed home nights. She thought of Chris Dawson,

and didn't consider her few dates with him in any way
constituting involvement, but—thank you, Chris—he'd
do.

'Well—not *heavily* involved,' she murmured.

And experienced another helping of astonishment
when, his expression stern almost, he had the nerve to
ask, 'Have you ever been "heavily" involved?'

The sauce! He was asking if she was a virgin! She was
positive he was! 'That's none of your business!' she
erupted angrily—and wanted to hit him again when, instead of being offended as he was meant to be, he
grinned. He actually grinned!

'You haven't!' he announced, and if her legs hadn't
felt so weak from that utterly bone-wilting grin she felt
sure she might have stood up and landed him one.

As it was she was left striving for as much nose-in-
the-air hauteur as she could find under the circumstances. 'We're getting away from the subject!' she stated
coldly, and realised her uppity manner had not gone
down well when he favoured her with a cool stare.

'The subject being that I should put my mother in a
situation which would force her to lie to her mother,' he
documented shortly.

She hated him again—he was refusing, she knew it.
'You don't care that I have to lie to mine!' she flared
back, and was momentarily diverted when he shrugged
and her glance was drawn to the magnificent hard-
muscled chest.

'You know the answer to that!'

What? Sabina dragged her gaze from his chest, her
head for an instant just so much cotton wool. Somehow,
though, she managed to collect herself, and to realise
that what Yorke was actually saying, as she had thought
he might, was that all she had to do was return that ring
and it would all be over.

'Oh, you!' she fumed impotently. And suddenly realising that she was going to get nowhere, that she could have saved herself the journey, she jerked off the bed, confused, only to experience yet more confusion on finding that Yorke had moved quickly and had caught hold of her wrist, to prevent her from storming back to her room.

'You came to talk—don't run away!' he grated.

She turned and stared, and while her heart started to thunder again she stared at him belligerently. 'I've said all I...' He truly had a most wonderful mouth. Oh, for goodness' sake!

Feeling impatient with herself, impatient with him, she turned swiftly and took a quick step towards the connecting door.

Unfortunately her bare feet somehow became tangled up in the bedclothes which Yorke had discarded during the night. And what with him still holding onto her wrist and refusing to let go, even so far as giving it a small tug, Sabina lost her balance.

One minute she was standing upright, about to charge back to her own room, and the next she was falling—but being saved by Yorke's grip. Only somehow, though she did not hit the floor, she landed, sort of catapulted, onto his bed.

For a moment she lay winded, finding she was staring up at him, the mattress at her back. Then she became aware that Yorke, while still sitting, was staring down at her. His mouth... Her anger disappeared—she couldn't for the moment remember why she had been angry.

She watched as his wonderful mouth picked up at the corners. And she supposed it was rather funny—she about to rocket from his room only to take a flying leap onto his bed.

Her own mouth started to curve upwards—she couldn't help it. It *was* funny and... Her mouth straightened. Yorke wasn't smiling. He was staring at her mouth as if magnetised.

Her lips parted; she felt she should say something. But her head seemed just so much cotton wool again, and she had nothing to say. But there was no need to say anything, because Yorke's head was coming down, and slowly, unhurriedly, he placed his wonderful mouth over hers.

Her heartbeats clamoured, but not in panic. His kiss was warm, gentle, and he had kissed her before.

But not like this! Gradually, causing her not the slightest alarm, the pressure of his kiss increased. He adjusted his position on the bed beside her, and she felt his strong arms come about her.

She had never known a man's arms could make her feel so warm, so secure, so safe. Yorke broke his kiss and as he looked down at her she stared back at him in a bemused kind of way.

'You don't seem particularly scared, sweet Sabina,' he murmured.

Was he hinting that she had cause to be? She could not believe it. 'I can be quite brave sometimes,' she smiled, and knew yet more bliss when his mouth tweaked a little in amusement and he bent his head.

Their lips met again and the intensity of his kiss deepened. She kissed him, responded fully, and as his arms around her tightened she realised that, while she had been kissed before, she had never been kissed before. That was to say no other kiss had ever made her feel the way that Yorke was starting to make her feel. She wanted to touch him.

His chest was over hers, and the next time he kissed her she just had to put her arms around him. 'Oh!' A sigh of sound escaped her. He was warm, his skin beneath her fingers a tingling delight.

At the small sound she made, Yorke took his mouth from hers and surveyed her seriously. 'I've an idea you don't do this every day,' he teased softly.

'I'm beginning to wonder why not,' she laughed, and loved it when he laughed too.

Then he was kissing her again, and as his mouth left hers he was kissing her throat, finding his way through the folds of her robe. Sabina felt his fingers at the tie belt. She knew he was going to undo it—and suddenly she didn't know how she felt about that.

Instinctively she put a hand down to halt him. He stopped immediately. 'No?' he questioned good-humouredly, his manner unhurried, gentle, a smile there for her. 'Apart from the fact you'll have steam coming out of your ears swathed in this thing, I want to feel you closer to me.'

Oh, heavens, she wanted to feel closer to him too; she couldn't deny it. 'I—um...' she murmured, and raised her head to kiss him.

And she in turn was kissed. He cupped his hands to her face, kissed her, buried his face in the tousled clouds of her hair, and kissed her again. And her need to be closer to him started to become urgent, and yet more urgent.

Barely knowing what she was doing, while Yorke's wonderful lips moulded to hers, she took her arms from him and sought out her tie belt and undid it. She then suffered a moment of shyness, but need not have worried because Yorke, aware of her every movement, aware of what she was doing, took over.

'You *are* brave,' he breathed, and kissed her, and, with his mouth holding hers, his hands went down to her towelling covering and he removed it from her.

'Yorke!' she gasped when, her robe disposed of, she felt the heat of his body against the skimpy length of her scrap of a cotton nightdress.

'Sabina,' he whispered, and kissed her, and tenderly caressed her arms and her back, and took her up to a higher plane of wanting.

She let her hands travel over his back, down to his waist, and, in a moment of urgent desire, knew not whether she was glad or sorry to find he seemed to have the sheet still about his bottom half.

She stroked his back, his shoulders, kissed him, was kissed, kissed his throat when he placed a whisper of kisses across her brow, and gripped onto him in a spasm of movement when his caressing hands moved to the front of her and he captured the swollen globes of her breasts.

'Oh!' broke from her.

'Relax, lovely Sabina; you've nothing to worry about,' Yorke smiled.

She smiled back, and tried not to clutch onto him a second time when he pushed the flimsy straps of her nightdress away and she felt his hands warm against the cotton covering the pulsating peaks of her breasts.

'I want to see you, to look at you,' he said, his voice thick in his throat.

'I—er—don't know that I'm—um—ready for that,' she breathed huskily, shyly.

'What do you know?' he teased.

I know I love you, she wanted to tell him. 'I... Kiss me,' she begged, and felt close to tears, her emotions were so overwhelming.

Yorke kissed her, and, as passion soared, mindless to what she was doing, she manoeuvred her nightdress down until her breasts were uncovered.

Again she wanted to tell Yorke of the joy of her love, but shyness kept her silent. Instead she put her arms up and around him and felt choked with emotion, with yearning, when she felt the touch of his naked chest against her uncovered breasts.

'Sweet love,' he groaned, and caressed her, moulding her breasts in his hands, teasing, touching the peaks until she was in an agony of wanting. Then, slowly, he levered himself slightly away from her and took his gaze from her face. 'You're beautiful,' he said on a breath of sound, his eyes on the delicious contours he had touched but not so far seen. And, as if he could not help himself, he bent his head, and kissed first one breast and then the other. And Sabina was reduced, seduced, into just holding onto him while his mouth and tongue and gentle teeth teased and tormented each hard, throbbing pink tip.

Sabina was in an agony of wanting when Yorke raised his head and placed his lips against hers. Soon, he would make her his—she knew he would, and it was what she wanted.

Or so she thought. But there were other barriers to be got through first, and even as one of his hands caressed down to her left thigh while with his other hand he freed himself from his only covering—the top bedsheet—nerves and shyness were bombarding her.

'Are you all right?' Yorke asked quietly, as if he'd got some sixth sense that she was feeling a hint jittery.

'I w-want you,' she replied, albeit her voice was a little wobbly. He smiled, and tenderly stroked her thigh. He moved nearer, his naked thigh positively scorching hers. 'B-but...' she stammered.

He stilled. 'But?' he questioned.

Oh, how she loved him. But he didn't love her. 'But—I...' Words failed her. 'No,' she said simply.

Yorke stared at her in some disbelief. 'No?' he echoed. Wordlessly, she shook her head. 'Well, that's one way to ruin a quite wonderful start to a Sunday morning,' he commented on a grunt of sound—and if she'd wanted proof that for him it was more lust than love, purely male appetite, then she guessed she had it. 'You're sure?'

'I'm—sure,' she choked.

And was unsure again when he moved from her, lay on his stomach and turned his head from her. She lay still, not wanting to leave, wanting to stay with him forever. 'Do you know something, Sabina?' his voice floated to her conversationally, for all she thought she detected a note of strain there.

'Wh-what?' she asked.

'Do you know that if you're not off this bed in another three seconds my self-control is going to be shot?'

'You mean...?'

'For God's sake! Do you want to be ravished?' he threatened.

Grief, there was definitely a note of strain there. Without another moment's thought Sabina rocketed from the bed. She was over by the door, about to go through it and already starting to feel mortified, when, perhaps from sheer bravado—she was too mixed up to be able to tell—she felt some parting words from her were needed.

'You couldn't ravish a flea off a rice pudding!' she jibed airily over her shoulder—but quickly got herself to the other side of the door and, as quickly, locked it.

Though whether it was to keep him out or to prevent herself from going back she was too het up to define.

CHAPTER SEVEN

IT TOOK until Monday for Sabina to fully accept that, yes, she was truly in love with Yorke Mackinnon. Even while hating him as she'd done her quick shopping trip on Saturday afternoon she had returned to Mulberry House—love making a liar of that hate. Quite simply, despite her belief that she was returning to Mulberry House for his grandmother's sake, it had, in truth, been Yorke that she wanted to spend more time with. She was in love with him, and there was absolutely nothing she could do to alter that. If wishing would do it, then it would be done—if only it were that easy.

Why, or how, she could have fallen in love with him was totally beyond her. As far as memory served, she had hated him more than she had liked him. It just did not make sense! Oh, he made her laugh, she'd give him that, but more often he made her angry, not to say furious—so why...?

The strength of her feelings when she had been in Yorke's arms still astonished her. Each time she recalled her early morning visit to his room she could feel herself going hot all over. She had been ready to forget everything—her upbringing, the fact that she wasn't even dating him, let alone committed to him in some way.

But for that last-minute reserve, that painful stab of memory that he did not love her she would have been his! Then what? Precisely—nothing! She had seen him once after that, but would not be seeing him again.

'Don't forget tomorrow night!' Chris Dawson reminded her when she bumped into him at work that day.

With her mind so much on trying to forget yesterday, it was only with a great deal of effort that she remembered she had a date with Chris tomorrow. 'I'm looking forward to it,' she smiled, her progress in telling untruths coming on in leaps and bounds. 'Where are we going?' Her conscience forced her to try and show some interest.

'There's a new place opened,' Chris replied, and chattily went on to tell her all about it.

From the sound of it, he had booked a table at some exclusive—and pricey—restaurant. It worried her. 'Um—look, you've paid the last couple of times we've been out. I really would like to treat you this time,' she suggested hopefully.

'Uh-uh.' He shook his head. But added, 'Though you can pay the time after if you like.'

'Good,' Sabina answered, and was back in her office by the time the reason for Chris Dawson's wide grin dawned on her. She had just agreed to go out with him again after tomorrow tonight!

She remembered somebody else's grin—a devastating grin—and Chris Dawson was forgotten. She was back in yesterday, back remembering how she had shot off the bed while she'd still had the emotional strength to do so. As now, she hadn't wanted to think then—so had gone straight to the bathroom and had turned on the shower.

And for an age she had stood beneath the shower trying to blank off thoughts that had not wanted to be blanked off. She was in love with Yorke Mackinnon—and much good would it do her.

Her one hope—one and only hope—lay in the possibility that the emotion she felt for him was purely physical. He was heady stuff, was Yorke. Grief, he'd only had to kiss her a few times and her backbone had turned to so much water!

There had not been a thought in her head that she had never been that far with any male of her acquaintance when Yorke had set about making her senses sing, so maybe she could put it all down to the physical. His tender, expert . . .

She had pulled herself together, reminding herself that since she was never going to see him again she would never have the opportunity to find out if there was a faint chance that it was merely physical.

Sabina had been out of the shower by that time, dried and dressed, with her damp hair tied back from her face in a rolled handkerchief. She had already decided that she was getting out of there. It was still earlyish, but no way did she want breakfast and, anticipating that Mrs Fairfax would, as a concession to her recent surgery, stay in bed a little longer than she would otherwise, Sabina had felt she could safely leave it to Yorke to make her excuses to his grandmother. He would know she had lit out anyway once he noticed the absence of her car on the drive.

Her belief that she would not see Yorke again before she left, however, received a setback when, in tidying her room and in gathering the day before's purchases together, she suddenly stopped dead. Oh, heavens, somehow or other she still had the nightdress she had bought in her possession—though how, when her last memory of it was that it had been somewhere around her waist— But, even while she was making a note to dump the nightdress the moment she got back to the apartment, she was searching around for the over-large towelling robe.

Whilst it would not have surprised her to find she had brought it with her back to her room, it did not surprise her either that she had not done so. And while a strong part of her urged, Oh, bubbles to it; let the housekeeper find it in Yorke's room—where she undoubtedly would

remember she had not placed it—something inside
Sabina would not allow her to leave it where Hazel
Evans, as sweet and pleasant as she was, would draw
her own conclusions.

Sabina's next dilemma was whether to wait until she
heard Yorke go from his room, when she could speed
in and retrieve it, or whether to go in anyway and scoop
it up—be it still on the bed.

Damn him—she was back to damning him again. She
wanted to be away. She didn't want to chance meeting
his grandmother again, and most certainly she didn't
want to see him again. So why didn't he get up and go
for a walk or something so she could get that robe and
get out of here?

Sabina was not terribly certain why she did not want
to be there when Mrs Fairfax got up, though she guessed
her guilty conscience and the fear that she might yet slip
up, might yet have to verbally lie to her, might have
something to do with it. But it was the thought of meeting
Yorke's grandmother again that prodded her into action.

On a spurt of courage she went swiftly to the communicating door. And there her courage faded. She
waited another thirty seconds and, thinking another annoyed, Damn him, had another spurt of courage—but
found it was not strong enough to make her unlock the
door and go in. It was strong enough to enable her to
rap sharply on the wood panelling, however. Though
she was an agitated mass inside as she turned back the
key and waited for her knock to be answered.

Fortunately, she did not have to wait long. And the
moment Yorke opened the door she was struck dumb.
He was shaved, showered—and wonderful, and she was
in love with him. Any hope she had nursed that her
emotions for him were purely physical went floating up
in smoke. She loved him—and any brief words she had
thought to say to him got stuck in her throat.

He, though, was not similarly afflicted. For, tall, stern, he stood there, taking in the sudden flush of colour that raced to her skin, and while she was starting to realise that she didn't care a light about that infernal robe and that she should never have knocked on the door—let the housekeeper think what she would—Yorke was stating shortly, caustically, 'You're not usually so polite.'

Rage shot through her. She wanted to hit him. How dared he so easily refer to the way she had, at five that morning—without stopping to knock—entered his room? She desperately wanted to say something biting in return—something to the effect that she had more about her than to want to barge in should he be in the middle of getting dressed—then recalled that he had been next door to naked the last time she had seen him!

She swallowed hard. 'May I have the robe I—?' She broke off, appalled that her voice should sound so husky. Yorke's look softened, but she didn't want him going gentle on her. She felt vulnerable—too vulnerable—and wanted—needed—to get out of there. 'I'm about to leave!' she stated bluntly, and was never more glad to hear she had found just the right sort of tart note.

'You're leaving!'

Sabina realised at once that she must have imagined a softening in him. For his tone then had been definitely hard-edged.

'Would you say my goodbyes to your grandm—?'

'Why the rush?' he snarled.

'I've a date!' she invented crossly. 'A date this afternoon.'

'His bed or yours?' Yorke barked furiously—and Sabina did what she had wanted to do for some while. She hit him.

His reaction was immediate. Firm, angry hands snaked out and caught her arms in a vice-like grip. But she was not going anywhere, and stood rooted, staring at him in astonishment. She had never hit anyone before—had not known she was going to do it then. It had just—happened. But even while Yorke's hands on her arms bit deep, as if he was striving for control, she was only capable of staring at him, at the livid mark on the side of his face that gave the reason why her right hand hurt.

It was obvious that Yorke did not take kindly to her attempt to fracture his cheekbone, yet, strangely, while she fully expected from the outrage in his expression that he would hit her back, or at least exact some sort of revenge, he from somewhere found the control he sought and, to her surprise, pushed her from him.

Sabina was still standing stupefied when a moment later he strode into his room and returned to thrust the robe at her, his manner curt, dismissive as he grated, 'You'll forgive me if I don't say it's been a pleasure!'

And that enraged her. Plainly he couldn't now wait for her to be gone. 'The pleasure was all mine!' she flew, and, aware he would know she was referring only to the satisfaction she had felt in hitting him, she slammed the door to. Pig! Swine! She hated him.

Her hatred of Yorke Mackinnon got her away from Mulberry House. But she was deeply in love with him again long before she arrived in London. Had she really hit him?

Sabina could still not quite believe it when Monday evening came around. She loved him, for goodness' sake, so how could she have struck him? She went to bed that night aware that since knowing Yorke Mackinnon everything she knew about herself had been stood on its head. Never would she have thought she could hit anyone, and certainly not anyone she cared deeply about, but she had. And what about that caution, that inbuilt reserve that was just so much part and parcel of her—where had that reserve been when Yorke had kissed her? When Yorke had...? Oh, my giddy aunt—the man had made a nonsense of her.

Sleep was elusive when, on top of everything else, her anxieties about Yorke's mother contacting her mother started to plague her again.

By morning, however, Yorke was back in her head with full force. It was then that she began to realise that there was no easy way to get him out of it.

'Seven o'clock all right?' Chris Dawson enquired when he stopped by her office to finalise their arrangements for that evening.

'Fine,' she smiled, and made every effort to look forward to the evening. You're going to enjoy it; you know you are.

To that end, not to mention that she was feeling guilty that she would just as soon stay home with a book, Sabina dressed with care that evening. She styled her night-black hair in an elegant, shining classic knot and donned one of her most expensive purchases—an elegant silk dress of deep violet.

She was rewarded by Chris's, 'Wow!' when he saw her. 'You look terrific!' he enthused. 'As you always do,' he added quickly.

'You don't look so bad yourself,' she smiled. She hadn't seen Chris in a dinner jacket before. He was tall and muscular and, while he wasn't Yorke, he wasn't bad-looking either.

The restaurant he took her to was everything it was said to be—quietly expensive and discreet, with a menu a gourmet would appreciate. It worried her a little that the cost of the evening would make quite a dent in Chris's wallet. But then she recalled some paperwork that had passed through her hands that day which had shown a person with Chris's expertise in the computer world could more or less name his own salary.

She started to relax, to cast small anxieties aside, and was even managing to forget about Yorke for two minutes together while she ate and chatted to Chris.

But Yorke was again in her thoughts when for no particular reason her glance was drawn to the right, where the head waiter was warmly greeting a pair of diners who had just come in.

No! She didn't believe it! She was seeing things! She blinked—but was not mistaken. It *was* Yorke. Her heartbeats crashed around. He had spotted her!

Her startled brown eyes met a pair of dark blue eyes— hastily she looked away. She strove desperately to look cool. Murphy's law dictated that of the two directions Yorke and his companion might choose to reach the only vacant table it would be the way that lay past the table where she and Chris were seated.

'What do you think of the wine?' Chris asked.

'Superb!' she answered. Yorke hadn't seemed very pleased to see her. In fact he'd looked positively disgruntled to see her there.

While Chris regaled her with the merits of the wine and where it came from, Sabina gave her thoughts over to how she wasn't going to so much as acknowledge that swine of a man—even if he gave her the chance.

She tilted her chin a fraction, inclining her head a trifle to the left. Ignoring was too good for him! She was aware of his presence, though. With every tingling nerve-end she was aware of him. Even as she smiled and replied Lord knew what to whatever Chris was going on about— something to do with a grape!—she was aware of Yorke.

And it *was* past their table that they came! Even with her head turned, her eyes on her dinner companion, she was aware of the head waiter leading the way past their table. She was not going to take a second look at the polished female following the head waiter either—that first sight of the tall, willowy, eaten-nothing-for-a-fortnight blonde had been enough to last her a lifetime.

Then Yorke was by their table. She refused to look at him. That was, even while her heart banged painfully against her ribs, she intended to ignore him completely.

So much for her intentions. She had known before that Yorke was not a man one could easily ignore. He made her intention impossible when, instead of following where the head waiter and his dinner companion led, he did no more than halt in his stride—right next to Sabina.

And, even as her thought processes went into zombie mode, Yorke, to her utter astonishment, did no more than bend down and with his warm mouth salute the side of her face!

Disbelieving, electrified, Sabina pulled back, away, her glance shooting to his. Casually, he straightened, his mouth—at odds with the cold look in his eyes—smiling warmly as he murmured, 'Can't stop, darling—wanted to remind you I'm waiting for a ring.'

With that, and without a scrap of acknowledgement to her dining partner—indeed barely seeming to have paused on his way to his table—her heightened awareness making everything go by in a kind of slow motion—Yorke went on his way. Swine! Swinish swine!

'*Who* was *that*?' Chris asked, slewing round in his chair to watch Yorke's departing back.

'Never saw him before in my life,' Sabina lied, willing Chris to go and slam Yorke over the head, *hard*, with the wine bottle.

Disappointingly, Chris remained where he was, and Sabina realised that for someone who had great problems when it came to telling an untruth she was growing quite accomplished at it.

'I'm waiting for a ring'! Huh! He could wait on! 'It seems I'm up against strong competition,' Chris murmured, accepting, it seemed, that there might be many acquaintances in her life who were waiting for her to give them a ring—to telephone them. And, while Sabina could have told him that Yorke wasn't one of them, and never would be, she was grateful to Chris that he was too much of a gentleman to suggest she had fibbed in declaring she didn't know the man who had kissed her cheek.

Her evening out with Chris might as well have been over then as far as Sabina was concerned. But it was not his fault that right at that moment all she wanted to do was to go home and get into bed and pull the covers up over her head—and stay there for a week.

Never had good manners been so called upon to get her through the remainder of the evening. She was aware of Yorke in the same room with every part of her—so how could she smile and chat to Chris as if she found him the most interesting man around?

Thankfully, they were at the end of their meal and Sabina did not have to endure for too long the torture of looking everywhere but at Yorke—not to mention at his tinkling-laughed companion.

She and Chris were on their way out, though, when, love being the exactor it was, it forced her to take a quick flick of a glance to Yorke's table.

He wasn't even looking! Indeed, he seemed so enamoured by his companion that it looked as if the ceiling would have to fall in before he would notice anything else.

'That was super!' she told Chris brightly on the way home.

And earned herself a 'Doing anything special this weekend?' prelude kind of question.

'My parents are expecting me.' She backed rapidly away, realising that, not being a total liar, she had just committed herself to spending the weekend in her old home.

'How about next week?' Chris asked as they reached her apartment block.

The answer to that was 'Bleak' but, having just spent a pleasantish evening with him, having told Chris it had been super, Sabina felt she could hardly now suggest that she would as soon stay at home.

'Do you like the theatre?' she asked. He, Yorke Mackinnon, wouldn't be staying home nights, would he?

'I do,' Chris affirmed hopefully.

'I'll get some tickets,' she smiled. And went indoors determining that she was *not* going to stay home nights. She would go out every chance she got. If Yorke Mackinnon thought she was going to stay home moping . . .

If Yorke Mackinnon thought? She must be going off her head! He hadn't space in his tall-willowy-blonde-filled life to give her another thought. Not that she wanted him to. No way did she want him, with his astute brain, wondering at the way she had reacted to him when he had kissed her on Sunday.

Oh, bother the man! Sabina started to derive more satisfaction from the fact that she had hit him. That should take care of any stray hint he might have given a second's thought to that she held him in any sort of loving regard.

Did he have any loving regard for his blonde companion? Jealousy bombarded her. Great searing, tormenting barbs of it. Was she special to him, the blonde? Sabina spent the next five minutes in excruciating torment. After which she managed to find a little relief in recalling how the blonde had been completely oblivious to the fact that her escort had paused on his way through the tables to kiss some other female—be it only on the cheek.

Sabina then immediately started to recall how, a few days earlier, Yorke had kissed her much more passionately. Surely a man truly in love—were he in love with the blonde—would not kiss another woman so? Why, had it not been for her calling a halt at the last minute then Yorke would have made her his, made complete love to her. And somehow Sabina felt that Yorke had more integrity than to make love to one woman while committed to another. The question was, was Yorke Mackinnon committed to his blonde dinner partner?

That question dogged her for most of the following day. If Yorke was committed though, why, after a business absence in Japan, would he spend the weekend not with the blonde but down at his grandmother's home in Warwickshire?

Well, he couldn't very well bring her with him, could he? Sabina argued. Not with his grandmother believing him to be engaged to somebody else.

At the end of her work day Sabina had done so much toing and froing over Yorke Mackinnon and his love-life that she went home feeling quite surprised she had managed to move such a workload.

She made herself something to eat, tried to think of something—someone—other than the man who seemed to occupy all of her thoughts, and wished yet again that Natalie would phone. Though how she was going to tell her over any phone call that her engagement ring had not been purchased by Rod Lacey but stolen by him Sabina did not know.

Sabina was still upset that her friend was going to have to know about Rod Lacey as she washed the dishes she had used, and she aimlessly returned to the sitting room feeling decidedly fed up.

With a long evening stretching before her, and in the interests of thinking of something else—Yorke Mackinnon was pushing to get into her head again—she

decided to take a shower, clean her teeth and give herself
a manicure.

Only her shower and teeth-cleaning had been achieved,
however, when the outer doorbell buzzed. Ridiculously
her thoughts went straight to Yorke—when did they not?
she thought irritatedly—and dismissed such nonsense to
wonder, since she was not expecting anyone, who it might
be.

Oliver, she concluded. He'd said something about
dropping a book in the last time she had seen him. Oliver
was an old friend. Old friends didn't need a specific
invitation.

Convinced it was her old friend, she picked up the
door phone. 'Oliver?' she enquired.

'Mmm,' he sort of grunted—she guessed he was having
problems over Melissa.

'Come up!' she invited, trying to inject a cheerful note
into her voice. No point in the two of them being down—
perhaps it would do her good to have someone to try
and cheer her up.

It was a very warm evening and had been another
sweltering day. She was wearing underwear and a many-
times-washed cotton wrap. She debated briefly about
going and getting dressed but apart from the time factor
Oliver came in the 'big brother' category, which ren-
dered her feeling comfortable with him however casually
dressed she was.

Her doorbell went, and that settled the matter. She
pinned a welcoming smile on her face and went to open
the door. And, on opening the door, her thinking patterns promptly went haywire.

'Who's Oliver that you should so warmly invite him
in looking like that?' Yorke Mackinnon snarled, his dark
gaze raking her slender being from head to foot.

Idiotically, she found herself stammering, 'H-he's seen
me w-without make-up before!' But, as her head started

to clear, so she forgot her scrubbed appearance and got angry. 'How dare you make me let you in by pretending to be someone else?'

'You're expecting Oliver?' he demanded, not a bit concerned at being taken to task.

'That's none of your business!' she retorted hotly, striving hard to be calm, realising she must have taken a few steps backwards because, without waiting for an invitation, Yorke had come through the doorway and had closed the door behind him.

'Is he the man you were with last night?' he wanted to know—as if that was any of his business either!

Going for Yorke's jugular had had no effect. Sabina took refuge in sarcasm. 'You should have hung around— I'd have introduced you,' she tossed at him sourly. She saw the corners of his mouth twitch—and even while angry with him she found that she wanted to laugh too. She gave up wondering what it was about him that he could have that effect on her—she loved him, and that was all there was to it. Yorke's smile never made it though, and Sabina stamped down hard on her impulses, and went on to demand, 'Well?' No reply—and not for the first time she felt she would dearly like to know what he was thinking. 'Look here, Mackinnon,' she fumed, exasperated, 'I'm busy. What do you want?'

Again she thought he was going to make her run for an answer. But, after long moments of scrutinising her, he forbore to state that, dressed as she was she looked busy, and drawled, 'I spotted your car parked by the garages as I drove near. I thought you might like to know—my grandmother thinks you're wonderful.' Then he smiled and Sabina's heart went into overdrive again.

Damn him and his charm. 'I'd have to be to put up with you!' she snapped, in desperate need of some backbone.

'Was—?' Yorke began, completely impervious to her short manner, it seemed, only to break off when her telephone started to ring. 'Answer it,' he suggested. 'I'll wait.'

Like blazes he would. Sabina had phoned her mother when she'd returned on Sunday, and was fairly certain it would be her mother on the other end of the phone now, ready for a lengthy mid-week chat. Oh, Lord— Yorke's mother hadn't been on the phone to her, had she? Sabina's anxieties about Yorke's mother contacting her mother were never very far away, but, as she already knew, she would be wasting her time asking his help.

She didn't have to put up with the bossy brute, though. 'I'll see you out,' she hinted, the door but a couple of yards away—and still the phone continued to ring.

'It might be Oliver saying he's been held up,' Yorke drawled.

'It could be,' she lied.

'Don't you think it's rather impolite not to talk to him?'

When had Yorke Mackinnon ever bothered about impolite? 'It would be far more impolite to talk to one boyfriend when my fiancé was within earshot!' Sabina offered drily, wishing her mother would hang up, and discovered that Yorke was fed up with the phone's clamouring too when, speaking as he moved, he went striding to her sitting room.

'Would you like me to—?'

'Don't you dare!' Sabina shrieked, chasing after him, realising, incredulously, that he intended answering her phone for her. Good grief—her mother's questions would be endless!

She caught up with him—though it was more that she cannoned into him when he halted abruptly when the phone suddenly stopped ringing. Yorke turned, taking

quick hold of her when it seemed she was going to fall
off balance.

'He means that much to you?' he grated malevolently.

Her heartbeats raced. His very touch was weakening.
'Not all men are swines!' she hurled at him. Oh, God—
he was marvellous.

'Swine or no—and dressed as you are for your boyfriend—no man has wakened you to the extent I...' But
Yorke had done with words.

He stared at her, gripped her as if striving for control—
and suddenly Sabina was unaware of anything very
much. And when Yorke's mouth met hers she just wasn't
thinking at all.

Strong arms were around her, Yorke was holding her
tight. She loved him, and kissed him back. Nor was one
kiss enough. Oh, how heavenly it was to be in his arms.
To be held by him. To be loved by him—but Yorke didn't
love her!

Sabina tried to push such thought away. She didn't
care that he didn't love her. It seemed a year since he
had last held her, since she had last been in his arms,
and she so desperately needed the solace of his arms, his
touch.

Yorke pulled her against him and Sabina willingly
moved closer to him. She felt his hard body against her
own, her thin clothing as nothing as he moulded her to
him.

She was drowning in her need of him when his mouth
left hers and, while his hands caressed her back, he trailed
gentle, tender kisses down the side of her throat.

With her head in such a whirl, her senses on fire for
him, it was a mystery to her why an annoying irritant
of the memory that he did not love her should rear its
unwanted head just as Yorke moved her thin covering
from her right shoulder.

She was all but mindless to anything save him as he traced a circle of feather-light kisses on the uncovered skin of her shoulder. So who was pulling her strings she had no idea—other than a wilful subconscious, which she would by far just then have preferred to have nothing to do with—when she suddenly jerked—pushed—and pulled out of his arms.

She even took a step back, when everything in her was crying out that she stay close. His arms fell away from her. He stared at her as if not quite believing her action either.

Yet that person in charge of her found more strength now that Yorke's firm and strong arms were no longer holding her. Even to the extent that, albeit there was a hint of staccato in her tones, Sabina heard that person that had taken charge state quite loftily, 'I agreed to be engaged to you—and nothing more. Would you mind leaving?'

He did not like her lofty attitude, she could tell, any more than he liked her words. And, when it came to arrogance, his arrogance beat her hollow. For, looking at her with a fire more of anger than of passion, Yorke all but floored her when, already on his way, he tossed at her toughly, 'When I want more than that from you, sweetheart, I'll let you know.'

Sabina didn't have to wonder what to do with the rest of the evening. No sooner did she hear the sound of the door closing behind him than she collapsed, devastated, into a chair.

She stayed like that for many hours. She did not need telling any more clearly that, though Yorke might on occasion—should the situation arise—find her physically desirable, it would be no more than that.

Painful though that knowledge was to live with, he had just made it very clear that, while he might enjoy a passing moment or two with her, he would always stay in control—and passing moments were all that anything that went on between them would amount to.

He would most certainly, as he had said, never want more than that from her. In fact, as he had just as good as stated, he would never, while he still had his sanity, fall in love with her. So why was it hurting so much? She had already known that.

CHAPTER EIGHT

LIFE went on, Sabina discovered. Even whilst she wanted to run away and hide like some wounded animal because all too painfully clearly Yorke wanted nothing from her, life went on.

Correction. Yorke wanted nothing from her but that ring. And that she could not give him. Again she fell to wishing that her friend would telephone but she had little hope that she would. Natalie, in love and loved, was journeying on an adventure with the only person she wanted to be with—London would be the last thing on her mind.

It was not without some trepidation that Sabina rang her mother early on Thursday evening. 'Hello, it's me!' she stated cheerfully.

'I tried to ring you last night,' her mother confirmed, and Sabina held her breath until her mother went on about some everyday topic. Yorke's mother was being very restrained, it seemed, and was, as he had requested, putting the congratulatory dinner on hold.

'All right if I come home this weekend?' Sabina requested.

'When have you ever had to ask?'

Sabina came away from the phone re-endorsing that the telephone wouldn't be good enough for her mother if she had so much as an inkling of what was going on. She would be over—jet-propelled.

Sabina was sleeping badly, and as day followed fractured night she began to despair. At times she felt she desperately wanted to see Yorke again yet was amazed at herself that, after his last comment, it should be so. At other times as her pride emerged, spiralled that she should be so weak, she wanted nothing more than to return that ring to him and let that be an end to it. That way she could start getting on with her life. She hated him and hated him, though, much more strongly, she loved him. And that ring was not hers to give to anybody until Natalie said so, and dear Natalie was always getting the sticky end—and life was a pill.

She went to her old home on Saturday, and felt a degree comforted to be with two people who loved her. Yet, at the same time, there was such a restlessness in her that every hour spent in her old home seemed to drag by endlessly.

She felt terribly ungrateful to be glad when the time came to go. But, having been at pains to hide her inner unhappiness, to try and carry on as if Yorke Mackinnon had never stormed into her life and turned her safe, cautious world upside down, Sabina knew a yearning to be on her own.

Yet nor did that suit. For once back in the apartment that early Sunday evening she seemed to be in a vacuum, and felt such a loneliness of spirit that she rang Oliver.

'Doing anything tonight?' she asked, not certain even as she spoke that she wanted to see Oliver either, but committed now.

'You haven't by any chance just come back from your parents'?'

'Hog!' she becalled him. 'I've got a raspberry tart.'

'I'm on my way!'

Sabina had the windows open and the sound of Oliver's sports car arrived in advance of him pressing the door buzzer, and she started to feel glad she had invited him over.

Melissa was yesterday's news, apparently, and Oliver was now keen on Tamara who was out of town next week—so was Sabina going to save his sanity by doing the decent thing and sparing him some of her time?

Sabina went out with Oliver on Monday and cooked for him on Tuesday. On Wednesday he invited her to dine at his place and since he did the cooking it was as well that she was off her food just then.

'Free tomorrow?' he enquired as she was leaving.

'I'm having my stomach pumped!' she replied, ducked a cushion, laughed and went home still heartsore and yearning for a glimpse of Yorke.

Sabina stayed home Thursday evening and, when she caught herself listening again and again for the sounds of someone at her door, could only be glad she had gone out the three previous evenings.

She had already told Oliver that she was going to the theatre with a man from her workplace on Friday. And was relieved when the next day dawned that it was so. For all her feelings of restlessness when she had been at her parents' home last weekend, she had an idea she might be heading that way again tomorrow. No way did she want to stay home, ears pitched for the sound of Yorke calling.

But he would never call again. She had known before that there was no need for them to see each other again unless she was ready to hand over that ring. That, Sabina realised, must have been the reason for his visit a week ago last Wednesday—eight and a half long, wearying, hungry-for-a-sight-of-him, aching days and nights ago. He had called to ask one final time for the return of his grandmother's ring—he most certainly hadn't called merely to tell her that his grandmother thought she was wonderful. That he had left without making that request for his grandmother's property was down to the fact that they had kissed... Sabina's thoughts drifted away.

'Perhaps we'll have a bit of dinner after the theatre,' Chris suggested when he stopped by her office that afternoon to insist he would call for her.

'That sounds nice,' she answered, and went home from work not keen on the theatre or a bite of dinner with him but finding consolation in the fact that it would all go to filling in a few more hours whilst she adjusted to living with this emotion which consumed her night and day.

The play was good. She tried hard to concentrate and, having many times pulled her thoughts back from Yorke, found she had retained enough of the plot to make a few intelligent remarks to Chris when at the end the lights went up and they started to file out.

'Now for some food,' he commented enthusiastically as they entered the foyer.

'Anywhere special in mind?' she queried, pushing out a cheerful smile because it was not his fault that he wasn't Yorke.

What Chris answered, though, she had no idea for just then she became aware of someone looking intently at her, and as she looked across so she recognised Dorothea Mackinnon!

Yorke's mother! What was she doing here? She should be at home in Surrey. Oh, grief! Sabina looked to the man with Mrs Mackinnon—as expected, it was Yorke's father.

Dying a dozen deaths, Sabina was never more grateful that with a crush of people trying to get to the way out she could neither have a conversation with Yorke's parents nor, as Dorothea Mackinnon's glance shot to Chris—clearly expecting her escort to be Yorke—was she called upon to introduce him.

She did not miss the way Yorke's mother frowned when Chris, seeing a gap for them to go through, put an arm about her shoulders to steer her that way.

Sabina smiled and waved, and wondered again at the recent complications to her more usual well-ordered life. Oh, heavens, what did she do now?

She started to grow all het up at the possibility that she might yet be called upon to introduce Chris. How on earth did she do that? What in creation would Chris's reaction be to any remark either of Yorke's parents might make to the effect that their son was engaged to her?

In the event, however, her fears were unwarranted because by some good and great fortune she did not spot Dorothea and Emmet Mackinnon again.

Even so, Sabina found it impossible to unwind. Even when panic receded, causing her to be able to reason that Yorke's parents had every right to come up from Surrey to go to the theatre once in a while—or twice for that matter if they felt like it—she was an inner mass of agitation.

Chris had thought to book a table in advance, but as they sat down to eat she had to own that her thoughts were very much elsewhere.

'Not very hungry?' he enquired, and Sabina pulled herself up short.

She just wasn't being fair to Chris. Why, she could barely remember saying a word to him this past half-hour. 'I'm saving myself for the pudding,' she told him cheerfully. 'Have you noticed the dessert trolley?'

He accepted it and she bucked her ideas up and, as much as she could, she put her private thoughts on hold until she could be by herself.

And an hour and a half later, in good humour, he drove her home to her apartment. 'Do I get to come in for coffee?'

'It's been a lovely evening, but...'

'But you don't want to spoil it and we've just had coffee?' Chris guessed.

'Some other time,' she prevaricated.

'It's getting better all the time,' he grinned, and stole a kiss just the same, and, having by the look of it assured himself of another date, he escorted her to her front door. 'Till next week, Sabina,' he said in parting, aware by then that she intended visiting her parents again that weekend.

'Till next week,' she agreed—and, wishing it could be otherwise, for she had grown to like him, she promptly forgot him as thoughts she had so far managed to keep at bay began to assault her.

Lord knew what Yorke's parents had thought when they'd seen her at the theatre with some other man. Some other man with his arm around her, she recalled. Oh, heavens! Should she warn him? Warn Yorke?

Warn Yorke? How? Why? Well, for one thing wasn't it only natural that his mother, or his father for that matter, should think it only right that their son should know his fiancée had been out with another man?

But Yorke was big enough to take care of himself, wasn't he? And after his last remarks to her he didn't deserve the slightest consideration, did he? And anyway... Oh, drat it. Regardless of what had gone on between them personally, surely it was only fair that she give him some sort of warning—alert him to be on his guard, to have some answer ready.

Yes, of course she had to warn him. Suddenly it seemed urgent somehow that since Yorke was as averse to telling lies to his parents as she was to hers she should give him the chance to have something ready to say when, as she was growing more positive would happen, one or other of his parents told him of having seen her at the theatre—and not alone.

Sabina started to feel shaky inside when she realised that any letter she wrote him with that information would not reach him until Monday. Oh—now what did she do?

She glanced at her watch. Most respectable people were in bed by now. So—what was wrong with waking him up? She quite liked the idea. Though it didn't seem so funny when it suddenly struck her that if she had thought to phone him then so might his parents have thought to phone him—a couple of hours ago!

The fact that they might not have—yet—decided her. She found his card with his private address and phone number on and, feeling all churned up inside, she began to stab out the digits. She felt even more churned up when his telephone started to ring out.

And ring and ring and ring. He couldn't sleep through the phone ringing, could he? Somehow she was convinced he was a light sleeper. She put the phone down, only to pick it up and press the redial button—and still no answer.

Was he abroad again? Somehow, and with no logic to it, she didn't believe that. What was more likely, she thought, feeling cross and sick at the same time, was that he was out on the town somewhere. It was a Friday night for goodness' sake, and Yorke was a very virile man.

She stopped her thoughts right there—didn't want to think further. Didn't want to think about the fact that he, right at this very minute, was out with some other woman. She fell to hoping that he was out at a midnight barbecue somewhere, and that the monsoons would come—it had been hot and sultry all day, with thunderstorms threatening.

Restlessly she prowled about the apartment with no thought in her head of going to bed. She tried the redial button again—with the same result as before.

Damn him, he didn't deserve that anyone should worry over warning him—out on the tiles all night! And yet she felt more than ever impelled to do so. Somehow it seemed imperative that she get to him before his mother did.

Drat him; drat that wretched ring. If it weren't for that item of jewellery, as beautiful as it was, she would now be tucked up in her bed fast asleep.

But she couldn't sleep, and the perimeters of her prowling about the apartment had extended to Natalie's room when Sabina obeyed a sudden impulse to go and look at that object that had caused so much trouble— and so much heartache.

It was beautiful, truly beautiful. If only... Her thoughts wandered off into the impossible and Sabina was in a make-believe world of being truly engaged to Yorke, with that terrible ache within her assuaged.

She came out of her brief reverie to find she was back in the sitting room with the ring now on her finger. It felt comfortable there. And even though it was not hers she did not want to take it off.

She sighed, and went over to the phone and again pressed the redial button. As before, he wasn't in. And she didn't care—let him go hang.

But she did care, and suddenly she had the idiotic idea of writing him a note. She could easily drive over to his address and push it through his letterbox for him to read when he *did* get in.

She dismissed the idea at once. Grief, she was going off her head! In all probability he *was* overseas somewhere. And if he wasn't overseas, then no way would he have an interest to read his mail when, at a quarter past lechery, he came home with some tall, willowy blonde on his arm.

Sabina decided to go to bed—but found instead that she was seated at a small writing desk by the window. OK, so she would write a note—but she wasn't going to deliver it to his address; she would post it. Let him squirm a bit when his mother phoned; it would do him good.

Bluntly she wrote that she had been to the theatre with a male friend—his parents had been there too. And that, while being unable to introduce her friend because of the crush, she had exchanged hand waves with his mother—Sabina could not remember Mrs Mackinnon smiling back.

Her letter written, Sabina placed it in an envelope and, love making her want to protect Yorke even while she was decidedly off him for the hours he kept, tried the redial button once more. Devil take it, it was almost half past one—and she was wide awake. In fact she had never felt less like going to sleep.

The night was silent and clammy when she went out to her car. Any minute now the heavens were going to open, she was sure of it. Not that she was worried; all she cared about was getting this letter delivered so that then perhaps she might start to feel sleepy.

Sabina found Yorke's smart address without any trouble. It was an elegant building in a salubrious area. She heard a rumble of thunder in the distance as she left her car, but so far the rain had held off.

There were a few steps to go up before she could make her way inside the exclusive apartment building. She had managed only one of them, however, when she heard the sound of footsteps behind.

She jerked round, some sixth sense seeming to warn her who it might be. 'Sabina!' Yorke exclaimed, halting so close to her that in the light from the lamps she could see into his face. He looked concerned. 'What's wrong?' he asked urgently.

For a moment, it seemed to her so much as though he really cared that at going on for two in the morning she was presenting herself on his doorstep with some cause for his concern that she could not answer.

'Come inside.' Yorke, as if suspecting she was in shock of some kind, took charge.

Sabina rather thought she was in shock—crazily she just had not expected to see him! Though why, when this was where he lived... Being in love must have sapped her brain power, she concluded, but could not deny the warm glow that assailed her that wherever he was, the tall, willowy blonde was not.

Suddenly, though, Sabina came to to become aware that, having nodded to the security desk on his way through, Yorke, with a hand on her arm, had led her through an elegant entrance hall and escorted her to a lift.

The lift was already floating upwards by the time she got her head together. 'Actually, there's nothing *too* wrong,' she blurted out in a hurry. Grief, why hadn't she just thrust her note at him and fled?

'That's a relief,' he smiled, was calm where she was all flustered inside. Oh, he was so, so... She loved his smile, she loved... 'Here we are,' he announced calmly, and suddenly Sabina felt no end of a fool.

'Look, I've blown it up out of all proportion,' she tried to excuse in a rush, wanting quite desperately to be out of there and back in her own apartment.

'Not to worry,' Yorke replied easily, guiding her from the lift and to his door. 'You'll allow me to make a sandwich for you at least,' he beguiled her as he unlocked the door and they entered his apartment with its tasteful furnishings.

She wanted to laugh, but did not know whether that was from what he said or from nerves. 'You're used to making sandwiches at this time of the night—morning?' she corrected.

'It depends,' he grinned, and oddly, even though the implication—it depended on what else he was doing— was obvious, Sabina found she was neither jealous nor cross but was enchanted.

'I've had dinner, actually,' she mentioned.

'You've been out,' he observed, his glance roving her stylish lightweight blue two-piece.

She sensed some sort of rebuke and didn't like it, though accepted that she was over-sensitive where he was concerned. 'So have you!' she retorted—and could have bitten out her tongue when he looked at her sharply. 'I tried to ring you,' she added lamely.

'Problem?' he enquired, but before she could tell him he invited, 'Have a seat.'

Since there was a sofa close by, it seemed a good idea. 'Not problem exactly...well, perhaps...' Good heavens, what was the matter with her—why didn't she just hand him that note and run for it? She watched as Yorke took his ease on the matching sofa opposite, and owned to feeling a touch more relaxed herself that he seemed in no rush to see her out. 'The thing is, I went to the theatre this evening, and...'

'Not dinner?'

'Theatre and dinner,' she amended. 'Do you have to dot every i and cross every t?' she demanded jumpily.

'You're nervous about something,' he rightly deduced, and she wanted to brain him.

'You know better than anyone that I'm not in the habit of calling on men at two in the morning!' she erupted to excuse her nervousness.

'You're not afraid I'll...?'

'Huh!' she scorned—and hated him when he laughed. 'I was coming out of the theatre,' she went on doggedly, 'when—'

'You were alone?'

Damn his eyes. 'Is that likely?' she scorned.

'Forgive me,' he apologised. 'Oliver?'

'Christopher actually,' she replied, losing it for a moment as she wondered what the blonde was called. Jealousy took a vicious swipe, and Sabina decided that she did not want to know. 'The thing is that as Chris and I were... I've written you a note; it's all there,' she sidetracked. 'I didn't expect to see you, but with you not answering your phone...?'

She had not been conscious of a question in her voice until Yorke willingly supplied, 'A business dinner—one of those that go on forever—and the need to walk it off afterwards.' A business dinner and a walk, regardless of the hour, afterwards! Oh, how wonderful. 'So,' he prodded, 'when I didn't answer my phone, you decided the matter was urgent enough to require you to drive over?'

'That's about it,' she replied, and quite forgot that she had been there some little while and still hadn't told him what it was yet.

Until Yorke further prompted, 'What matter would this be, Sabina?'

Oh, grief, it really was getting to her. 'The matter of your parents choosing the same theatre for their Friday night's entertainment,' she said in a rush.

There was no need for her to elaborate; Yorke got the picture straight away. 'Did you introduce your escort?' he questioned.

'We didn't get to speak. We were on our way out. It was a bit of a crush with everyone making for the exit, so...'

'My parents knew you were with this man?'

'They couldn't be off knowing. Chris had his arm around me, and—' She didn't get to finish because, his expression darkening on the instant, Yorke was slicing her off.

'You're usually so demonstrative in public?' he snarled—and she stared at him, stunned—but not for long!

'Oh, go to hell!' she flared, what with nerves biting, on her feet and angry too. 'I wish I hadn't come!' she exploded, her eyes going to the door. 'I wouldn't have

done but for some misguided notion that I should warn
you.'

Yorke did not thank her, but instead was all aggressiveness when, to her amazement, he roared, 'If you'd
done the decent thing and stopped dating whilst you're
engaged to me, you wouldn't have a need to warn me
of anything!'

Sabina looked at him, flabbergasted. God . . . he really
was the end. 'I'm not engaged to you!' she erupted when
she got her breath back.

'You're wearing my ring!' he shot her a fast ricochet.

Oh, God—she had forgotten! But trust him to notice!
Sabina felt her cheeks go mortifyingly hot—and she came
the closest ever to throwing the ring at him and getting
out of there.

'It's not your ring, anyway,' was the best defence she
could think of at that moment. But, as jealousy took
another swipe, she found more defence as she attacked,
'I don't suppose you've given up all your women just
because of *our* "engagement".'

Almost toe to toe, they glared at each other. Talk your
way out of that, she silently fumed. He knew that she
knew he'd been toting a blonde around since their
'engagement'.

Her feelings of mutiny against him, however, were
suddenly sent flying when, albeit he favoured her with
a short-tempered look, Yorke actually offered, 'I will if
you will.'

Sabina stared at him, her eyes huge in her face. Surely
for him to be so ready to give up his freedom to date
where he would for the duration of their 'engagement'—
with no idea of when it would end—had to mean that
he was not heavily involved with anyone?

So cheered was she by that thought that she was ready
to at once state unequivocally that she would not see
anyone until their 'engagement' had been resolved. She

even opened her mouth to say so—then suddenly began to feel so vulnerable, so wide open, so much in love—and so without a defence—that all she knew was that she must leave—and now.

'Forget it,' she snapped haughtily, and went to move quickly past him.

Yorke was quicker. 'Have you told him about us?' he demanded, a hand shooting out to take an iron grip of her arm and prevent her going anywhere until he was good and ready.

Sabina threw him a hostile look. There was no 'us'. But clearly he was seriously angry with her and her arrogant manner, and was having none of it. Well, tough! Though on looking at him Sabina could tell from the steely glint in his eyes that she would be wasting her time to demand that he let her go.

She opted for more arrogance instead. 'Which one should I tell, Chris or Oliver?' she challenged loftily, and knew as the iron grip on her tightened yet more firmly that she had gone too far.

'Whoever!' he snarled, and, every bit as perceptive as she knew him to be, added, 'Though none of them can make you respond the way you do to me, can they?'

That terrified her! Oh, my heavens, did he know? Had he guessed? 'As if!' she jibed—that or die.

'Trying to deny it?' he jeered—and gave her no time to think up an answer, because he at once set about proving his theory.

Sabina was still striving for wit, for coherence when Yorke pulled her hard up against him and, both his arms now about her, laid his lips against hers in a hard, brutal kiss.

She pushed at him, tried to get free. She did not want to be kissed like this. 'Get away from me!' she demanded when she had charge of her own mouth again.

'Pretending you don't like it?' he taunted, and she hated him and kicked out at him—all to no avail, for his lips were again on hers.

'You misbegotten...' she began to yell, when she again had freedom to say anything.

'Compliments, compliments,' he derided, and kissed her again.

She kicked him. He didn't like it, and it did nothing to sweeten him. But if she had been looking to make him break his hold, looking to make her escape, then she found she had done just the reverse. Because one minute she was hard up against him—vertical—and the next she was hard beneath him—horizontal—on the sofa.

He was strong, and she hated him, hated him that with his weight over her she was powerless. 'I never took you as a rapist!' she found enough spirit to fire.

'I never took you,' he answered meaningfully. 'Perhaps I should have when I had the chance.'

She so very nearly gave him another, 'As if!' but immediately realised that that would, in these circumstances, be much too provocative. 'You're—hurting me,' she said instead, and was a mixture of surprise and relief when he straight away, while still keeping her his prisoner, moved his weight to the side of her.

Sabina was well on to realising what she had instinctively known all along—that Yorke had no plan to rape her—when his mouth sought and found hers again. No, no, she didn't want to be kissed in this way, this... Suddenly, Yorke's kisses began to change. His mouth wasn't hard and brutal against hers but his lips tender, seeking...

She was confused. She twisted her head. The kiss was broken. Yet she felt compelled to turn her head back. She looked at him, at that face so close to hers, all aggression gone. He looked back, those dark eyes searching

her face. Then his head was closer again—she closed her
eyes.

Sabina had no idea when she had stopped fighting;
all she knew as Yorke sprinkled tender kisses on her face
and eyes was that while she had been unafraid of his
toughness it had been gentleness that had totally dis-
armed her.

She had no idea either of quite when she had started
to kiss him back, to respond. What she did know was
that it was heaven, that to be in his arms again was a
salve to all her aching longing.

Far from being ready to kick and punch and push,
she now held onto him as he traced butterfly kisses down
the side of her neck, and adored him when his lips,
teasing hers apart, again met hers.

She luxuriated in the feel of his body against hers—
where his jacket had gone to she had not the vaguest
idea—and, when he began to unbutton the top of her
two-piece, so she began—for her, outrageously unin-
hibited—to unbutton his shirt.

'Oh,' she sighed when her handiwork revealed his
broad chest.

Obligingly he shrugged out of his shirt, and her delight was endless as her fingers caressed and cavorted
over muscle and in hair and in just the sheer maleness
of the man she loved.

Then she was mindless of everything as tenderly Yorke
removed her jacket and bra, and, kissing and caressing
her in turn, he pulled her close, his naked chest burning
the firm mounds of her breasts.

'Oh,' she breathed.

'You're exquisite,' Yorke murmured, and as she
drowned in his words so he kissed her lips, and then
moved to kiss and mould her breasts, and to take her to
a pinnacle of wanting such as she had never known. Her

heartbeats thundered and she was in a sublime no man's land of love.

Wantonly she would not have cared had he removed the rest of her clothing. Indeed, as a fire roared in her, out of control, she felt she would have welcomed such removal.

But, even while he kissed her eyes, the side of her nose, and finally laid his lips on hers, while gently his right hand cupped, moulded and deliciously tormented the hardened pink tip, so she sensed a change come about him.

'What...?' she whispered when he stilled—all his, wishing, wanting to be his—with no thought in her head to back away when the time came, as soon it must.

Yorke took his mouth from hers, staring down at her. He seemed somehow—disturbed about something as he took his gaze from her face. She watched as he raised himself from her, saw him stare down at her naked breasts—and had no notion what was going through his mind as, slowly, he shook his head.

Whether he shook his head in denial or merely to clear it, Sabina had no way of knowing. But, with her eyes fixed on his face, dread started to enter her pounding heart. He was unsmiling, and she had no idea why.

'Yorke?' She called his name softly.

'No!' he replied sharply, denying himself, denying her, and she just did not understand.

'No, you don't w-want...?' My God, was this her begging a man to make love to her? It was, it seemed. Nor could she stop. Her pride had dissolved without trace. For, even as he sat up, presented her with his back and began to shrug into his shirt, she heard herself plead, 'Did I do something wrong? I'm sorry, I know I'm not very experienced, but—'

'Tell me something I don't know!' he clipped.

His tone wounded her. Yet still she could not give up. 'What did I do?' She still wasn't ready to accept what was staring her in the face—that Yorke had no intention of making love to her; that he somehow—and she had no idea how, why—had gone totally off the idea of making her his.

'Put your clothes on,' he snarled—and only then did her pride come hurtling back. Great shaming lorry-loads of it.

'Why should I?' she flew. 'You took them off!'

'My mistake,' he grated, and got up and walked away.

'You're exquisite,' he'd said—and she'd believed him! Believed in that underlying passion in his voice. My God, what had this man done to her? 'No—the mistake was all mine!' she retorted shakily, amazed as she attempted to get into her clothes that she was trembling so much she could barely do up her bra. She was on her feet, making a fist of doing up the buttons on her jacket, searching for her shoes, when Yorke turned about. 'I made a mistake in coming here—but that's soon remedied,' she went on snappily, barely recognising that out-of-control voice as her own, and, finding her shoes, she thrust her feet into them, picked up her bag, and had taken a step towards the door when Yorke, moving to stand in front of her, stopped her.

'Where do you think you're going?' he questioned, nothing lover-like about him now as he stared hostilely at her.

'Strange as it may seem, I've gone off the idea of sharing your bed. If it's all the same to you, I'm going home to mine!' Thank heavens for sarcasm—it was that or tears—and she'd suffered enough shame and humiliation for one night. For him to see her in tears would be the end.

'Not in this, you're not!' Yorke retorted toughly, no question about it.

'This?' As she spoke so Sabina suddenly became aware that the weather had broken, and that with thunder, lightning, not to mention a cloud-burst or two, all hell was breaking loose out there. It seemed incredible that anyone could be mindless to such a storm crashing around—she guessed she had him to thank for that! A drive home in such conditions, however, was the least of her worries just then. 'Out of my way!' she ordered. 'I'll swim it if I have to.'

'You can forget that!' he decreed, and, ignoring her order, said, 'You can have the spare bedroom. You'll—'

'Stuff your spare bedroom!' she politely turned down his invitation—and was around him and off.

Yorke was at the door before her. 'Look at you,' he exploded. 'You're shaking all over! You're in no condition to drive.'

He was right, and because he was right and was too big to push away from that door she hated him that she had to accept that he was right. 'Don't bring me breakfast in bed!' she spat, moving away from the door. 'In fact, don't ever come near me again!'

She had been in the solitary confinement of the room he had shown her for all of ten minutes before the crassness of her last remark came back to haunt her. 'Don't ever come near me again'? Grief—Yorke had shown in no doubting manner that he was bitterly regretting having kissed her—and that the sky would fall in before there would ever be the remotest likelihood of him doing so again.

The next hour dragged by on leaden feet. She had no intention of going to bed. It was pointless anyhow—she was too emotionally upset to be able to sleep. Pointless, too, to go over and over everything again—but she did not seem able to stop.

She had been too willing. Painful to accept that, but it was true. Willing, and foolish—she had all but screamed at him to make her his. And he, a man who made difficult decisions every day, would have no interest in anything so easy.

Her cheeks flamed at that last thought. Easy! She did not like it—but could not deny she had been willing, eager...

But how else should she be? She searched for a defence. She loved him. Oh, grief—had Yorke seen her love for him! Was that what had put him off? Oh, no, she couldn't bear it! It was the end. She knew it, and she wanted out.

Sabina was still going under with mortification as the first fingers of dawn started to filter through the night sky. The way she had been with him! And she still wanted him. And not just sexually. And, heaven help her, Yorke was worldly enough to know that. It was no good at all telling herself that he had not been averse to a little love-making... *Little!* She had never thought herself capable of such ardour.

The storm of the night had gone but the storm of embarrassment she carried was threatening to sink her when two minutes later, taking the greatest care not to make the smallest sound, she left the guest bedroom.

She was out in the hall when she at last accepted that which was staring her in the face. This was the end. She would not see Yorke again. The words 'This is the end' spun around in her head. And she now knew that she had to be the one to end it.

There was a small antique table by the door. Not allowing herself to think about it, Sabina slipped the engagement ring from her finger. Under the cover of a siren-sounding ambulance going by, she placed the ring on the table and silently let herself out of the apartment.

She was driving to Natalie's apartment, not daring to let herself think of Natalie and the way she had stolen from her that ring which had been stolen in the first place, when more embarrassment showered her. For only then, in the cold light of day, was she able to see that last night that void, that ache in her for Yorke, had been so bad that she had been looking for an excuse to have some contact with him!

Dreadful though it was, shaming though it was, totally without pride though it was, only now was it blatantly obvious that Yorke would cope with whatever was thrown at him! There had been no need to try to phone, to write, to drive to warn him!

Sabina let herself into the apartment and went straight to bed. She slept for a couple of hours but was up again, showered and dressed by seven-thirty.

She was expected at her parents' home today but had gone beyond loneliness of spirit and would rather not go.

Yorke pushed his way into her thoughts again—so much for her trying to keep him out. Still, she was glad she had ended it—she refused to listen to the voice that asked who she was attempting to fool. Far better when Yorke returned that ring to its rightful owner for him to say that his 'engagement' was broken than for him to have to tell his grandmother that her other grandson had stolen it.

And, tact being the name of the game, neither his father nor his mother was likely to mention their son's brief engagement to either of her parents at any time.

Sabina wasn't hungry, but she made herself a cup of tea. Though after a few minutes of staring into space with thoughts she did not want chasing one after the other around in her brain she jumped up, feeling claustrophobic suddenly, and decided to take a walk to the paper shop.

She had never felt so down, and couldn't have said that she felt any better on her return journey. But on stopping by her mail box—she had all but given up expecting another card from Natalie—she discovered a little light in her darkness in that there was something for her with a Brazilian stamp on it. Nor was it merely a postcard but Natalie had written her a letter.

Feeling a degree or two uplifted, Sabina took the letter up to the apartment. She slit open the envelope and, anticipating pinning her thoughts on something else for a few minutes, she began to read of the adventures which Natalie and Rod were experiencing. It was as she came to the last page of Natalie's long and interesting letter, however, that Sabina's eyes began to widen—in shock! Natalie had written:

Talk about putting the cart before the horse! I should have started this letter with an apology. But, what with everything between Rod and me being so absolutely sublime—I just can't express how happy I am, Sabbie—I've all but forgotten that some weeks ago Rod and I came within an nth of splitting up.

Oh, dear. Sabina wondered what had gone on—and very near dropped on the spot when she found out.

By now—three weeks ago, I expect—Rod's cousin, Yorke Mackinnon, will have been in touch with you and will have shown you my handwritten assurance in Rod's letter to him that it was all right for you to hand over my gorgeous engagement ring.

Sabina blinked, and read that last part again—taking into account the postal service, over three weeks ago Natalie had given permission for her to hand over that wretched, wretched, heartbreaking ring!

She carried on reading.

Honestly, I just couldn't believe it when—it was the day after I'd sent you a card saying how fantastic everything was between us—that, admittedly after a few glasses of excellent French wine, Rod confessed how he hadn't exactly purchased my engagement ring but had "borrowed" it. I was, as you can imagine, instantly sober, appalled and angry. Apart from anything else, how *could* he expect me to wear something he had stolen? We had a blazing row which ended in my telling him he could forget about being on the same plane as me to Brazil the next day. I'll spare you the details of the fight but the outcome was Rod's letter to his cousin—with my written endorsement—the very next morning. We put it in the post together before we left France. I can't tell you how terrific life is— I'm in danger of going soppy again—but never did I think anyone would love me the way Rod has shown that he does.

There was more about the small ways in which Rod showed that he cared, but Sabina, while heartily relieved that Rod himself had confessed about his grandmother's ring, was too stunned to appreciate more than that—ye gods—three weeks ago—*three weeks ago*!— Yorke had received a letter from Rod Lacey which included Natalie's permission for her to give him that ring!

Minutes ticked by while Sabina read, read again, and then reread what Natalie had written—and still she could not believe that for the last two weeks Yorke Mackinnon—when she had seen him several times in that period—had not said a word to her!

Why? Why? Why? buzzed around in her brain as she realised that he must have already received his cousin's letter the other Saturday when he had turned up and found her at his grandmother's home. Was it fury with her, fury to find her there, that had made him decide to say nothing about it?

Try as she might, Sabina couldn't see any sense in that. For, had he said anything, she could have gone quietly home—their 'engagement' at an end.

Then she remembered the Sunday morning after that Saturday, and how, in the early hours, she had gone to his room with the idea of getting him to see to it that his parents said not a word to her parents about their 'engagement'—yet, all the time, he had known that he had only to show her Rod's letter and that would be an end to it!

Sabina started to grow angry. Particularly did she grow angry when she recalled, entirely without effort—it was after all seared into her memory—how Yorke had started to make love to her, and had damn near succeeded in making her his.

My stars, he must have been laughing his socks off the whole time. Not that he'd been wearing any then—or much else either. Sabina pushed such unwanted pictures from her. Why? To punish her, to take retribution for her daring to defy him when he'd demanded the return of that ring? To pay her out for her nerve?

None of it made any sense, the only salient fact being that *two weeks ago* it could all have been ended! Damn him, damn him to hell! Sabina had no idea what sort of game Yorke was playing but she didn't thank him for the emotional trauma she had endured. Nor the fear she had known when trying to protect her protective parents from hearing about her 'engagement'. Not to mention her anxiety about that ring and its rightful owner in relation to Natalie and everyone letting her down.

And Sabina thanked him not at all that, through being unaware that Natalie had long since given permission for her to hand that ring over, she had felt sick with herself ever since she had left that ring on Yorke's hall table this morning.

The man wanted putting down, she fumed angrily. No wonder he'd been able to talk so readily of giving up his dates during the time of their 'engagement'—he'd darn well known he could cancel their 'engagement' any time he felt like it. Though why he should want her not to date anybody was a mystery to her.

Her anger went from mere anger to total fury. He was a lordly, arrogant, double-dealing swine. And but for the fact that she had gone to see him last night, only to painfully analyse the true reason for that on her way home this morning, she would have charged over there and told him a few home truths.

But, having suffered from badly bruised and damaged pride, the more Sabina thought of Yorke Mackinnon's treachery of silence, the more enraged she became. Her pride surfaced. Whole and complete. Great giant swathes of it. Who the hell *did* he think he was? Then the outer door buzzer went.

Oh, bother it! She wouldn't answer it. She was in no mood to see Oliver, good friend though he was. The buzzer sounded again—impatiently. Oh, devil take it—ten to one he'd seen her car. He had more than likely, as was his wont, parked his Morgan just behind it.

The buzzer went again—for longer this time—and even while she sighed and wondered about good friends—for only good friends would think of calling at this early hour of a Saturday morning without prior arrangement—Sabina went and answered the intercom.

'Yes,' she said, hoping, much though she was fond of Oliver, that her tone would put him off—she had her own problems without taking on any he might be having with Tamara.

'Yorke,' came the answer! And she just did not believe it!

'Yorke—of Mackinnon fame?' she questioned tautly, her fury with him returning with a vengeance.

'The same,' he clipped.

My God, was there no end to his nerve? He'd got that ring—what else was there? From his curt, determined kind of tone, it didn't sound as though he'd come to apologise.

And that made her mad too. In her book, she was owed one very big apology. 'What do *you* want?' she charged snappily, wanting to physically set about him.

'I want to talk to you.'

Sabina was angry enough to have any conversation there was to be had through the intercom. That way she could shut him off whenever she felt like it.

But in her view she had humiliated herself enough. As far as she was concerned it was now all ended. But if that rat out there wanted to add a postscript, then she would handle it with more dignity than that.

She pressed the door-release mechanism—and waited.

CHAPTER NINE

SHE did not have to wait long before Yorke was ringing her doorbell. With the light of battle in her eyes, Sabina went to let him in—but did not know whether it was fury, anxiety or just love for the deceiving swine that caused her to start inwardly trembling the moment she saw him.

Fearing her voice might come out sounding much less hating than she wanted it, without a word she came away from the door. She knew he had followed her when she heard the decisive click as he closed the door, but oddly she felt a shade on shaky ground because there seemed something very determined about it, and him.

This was ridiculous. He was at fault, not her. Sabina snapped out of it sharply and spun round to face him. She hadn't been mistaken about the determination— there was a purposeful glint in his dark blue eyes. Who did he think he was?

'So talk,' she invited uninvitingly, tilting her chin so he should know in advance that he might just as well save his breath.

'You're angry with me for some reason?' The utter gall of him! Oh, for an axe!

She swallowed hard—that or hit him. 'It's not every day I get taken for a ride!' she retorted shortly. Dignity, dignity; for heaven's sake, try to keep your dignity.

'Ride?' he queried, and shin-kicking tendencies reawakened in her.

Dignity—she strove for dignity. 'I'm not interested in lies,' she erupted angrily, striving hard for calm. 'Nor, for that matter, in anything you have to say.' Why then had she allowed him to come up? Sabina ignored the torment of logic; she didn't need it. 'You've got what you've been after all these weeks, so—'

'In actual fact, I haven't.' Yorke cut through what she was saying. 'I—'

'Didn't you find it? I left it on the—'

'I found the ring,' he cut in as she started to feel uneasily that his grandmother's ring had somehow got lost. 'But that isn't what I want.'

'You could have fooled me!' Sabina flared—but in spite of herself, and despite her present hate for him, weak though she owned she was, she was intrigued to know more. Not that she'd ask—she'd die sooner. 'You could have h-had me too, so it isn't that either.'

'You're blushing again,' Yorke commented kindly.

'Oh—go to hell!' she blazed, and turned her back on him.

'I feel as though I'm already halfway there,' he stated. He sounded closer than she had thought.

'How?' she asked, not meaning to at all. 'Don't answer that—I'm not interested!' she erupted, turning about. He was close! Had moved to close the gap. She backed away and was on an emotional see-saw of doing her best to stay calm and dignified but constantly failing.

'I was afraid of that,' Yorke replied solemnly, and that took Sabina out of her stride again—she had never supposed him to be afraid of anything. It puzzled her. Was he actually saying that he was afraid that she was not interested?

In what, for goodness' sake? Oh, grow up. He was clever, was Yorke, and could run rings around her. What he was up to now was beyond her. But was she just to stand there and put up with it?

'I take it your conscience kept you awake!' she went on to the attack to offer sarcastically in a not so oblique reference to the earliness of his visit.

'It's true I haven't been sleeping well of late,' he admitted.

Join the club! 'With all you've got to weigh you down I'm not in the least surprised,' she let fly.

Yorke looked from her, though whether to decide if he should agree or not she could not tell. But, watching him closely, she saw his glance light on the coffee-table. It had an envelope on it—that envelope bearing a Brazilian stamp. He looked sharply up, and she knew that, in an instant, he had got the picture.

Any decision he might have made to agree he had a lot on his conscience was in that instant lost. 'You've heard from Natalie?' he abruptly questioned—already knowing the answer to that one.

'As you've heard from Rod Lacey!' Sabina snapped, glad to feel angry again. 'The difference is,' she surged on when he opened his mouth to speak, 'that, while I received my letter only this morning, you received your letter some weeks ago.'

Yorke silently stared at her, observing the heat of anger in her cheeks, the sparks of fury in her large brown eyes. 'I—confess it,' he quietly agreed at length.

'Big of you! Now will you please go? I've things to do today that don't include you.'

'We've things to talk about.'

'Correction—you've things to talk about; I—as I might have mentioned—am not interested.' Sabina denied the weakness invading of not wanting him to go, never wanting him to go—but contrarily of wanting him to go while she was still strong enough to refuse to listen to him. Yorke's look on her was unsmiling. She stared, unsmiling, back—so why, when she was firmly refusing to budge from her 'not interested' stance, should the traitor in her demand, albeit tartly, 'What's to discuss, anyway? You've dec—'

'More than you know.' Yorke was in before she could go on to tell him what a deceiving rat he was. 'Look,' he followed up, refusing to let her get in again, 'why don't we sit down and discuss, as rationally as we can—?'

'How you *knew, ages ago*, that...?' Her voice faded. Was Yorke, with his talk of 'as rationally as *we* can' intimating that, while he considered that she was irrational, he was not feeling all that rational about the things—matter—which he wanted to discuss either? My stars—that was a first! And she didn't believe it anyway. Just the same, it unnerved her a jot. 'Er...' she went to go on, but, and against everything in her head to the contrary, she suddenly felt that to sit down might not be a bad idea. She went to the nearest chair, indicating that he should do likewise, though warned, as he seated his long length, 'Don't get too comfortable!'

Oh, God, he made her insides go all weak when he allowed that suspicion of a smile to tweak the corners of his mouth at her unveiled hint that he wouldn't be stopping long.

'So, what did *your* letter say?' she demanded frostily— anything to counteract that weakness in her that knew no pride.

'I have it here,' Yorke replied, and, reaching into his pocket, took it out and, their two chairs being close enough, stretched out and handed it to her.

That surprised her. Oh, where the devil was her backbone? She took the letter from him, but didn't see why she should be pleasant about it. 'You'll be saying next that you brought it with you to show me!' she remarked waspishly.

'I did,' he agreed.

In her view, he was being far too agreeable—it wasn't like him. 'Bit late in the day, wouldn't you say? You already have the ring.'

'It is late in the day, as you've said,' he again agreed. 'And I've been more than remiss in not showing you that letter before now. But I want everything out in the open between us now, Sabina, so—'

Tough! 'Remiss!' She latched onto that one word, the letter in her hand forgotten. 'That's an easy word to use considering the trauma I've been through worrying about your parents getting in touch with mine!'

'Oh, I knew that they wouldn't do that,' Yorke answered confidently, adding, unbelievably, 'My father's far too busy at the moment to have time to play golf, and I'm certain my mother wouldn't dream of contacting your mother without first mentioning it to me.'

'I'm glad you're so certain. I wish you'd confided that certainty in me!' Sabina erupted. 'I came specially to your bedroom down at Mulberry House to ask you to tell your parents the truth. I told you I couldn't lie to my parents. I—'

'And I,' Yorke gently inserted, 'was all set to tell you the truth—only we kissed—and I wasn't thinking very clearly for a long while after that.'

'You...' She wanted more words, but none would come. She remembered being in his arms, being kissed by him. It had been wonderful. She hadn't been thinking at all when she had lain in his arms—but—had it been like that for him too? She shook her head and didn't believe it. Yorke was a man of the world, and had probably been in that situation dozens of times—and remained thinking and in control. 'Yes, well, getting back to this letter,' she said hurriedly, trying to grab some of her cotton-wool thoughts together. 'You knew, the day before, on that Saturday when you drove down to your grandmother's, that we could end our "engagement" straight away. You knew that you had only to show me Rod's letter, the part Natalie wrote in it, and I would give you that ring then and there. You did know then? You did have Rod's letter by then?' she insisted on knowing, not certain she would believe him if he answered no.

But he did not answer no, but at once owned, 'I returned home from Japan early that morning—my cousin's letter was waiting for me.' Sparks started to flash in her eyes again at his blatant confession. Only for her anger to dip when Yorke promptly followed up by adding, 'As too was a message from my PA to say that you'd been in touch wanting my grandmother's phone number.'

'You know why!' Sabina refused to defend herself, though irritatingly found she was tacking on, 'What was I supposed to do, leave her there waiting?'

'Not you, Sabina. You're much too sensitive for that.'

Sabina stared at him. Had she heard him rightly? Her heart skipped a beat. Grief, Yorke made it sound as if he liked that about her. 'Well...' she began, and for a moment was stumped. That was before she recalled the way it had been. 'Well, you didn't say that at the time!' she challenged. 'You were as mad as hell when you turned up at your grandmother's and found me there.'

'My sins are endless,' Yorke stated, ready, it seemed, to agree with anything she threw at him, that charm she found so devastating there again. 'Though, prior to my going down to Mulberry House, I had tried to phone you—and drove over here too on the off chance of seeing you.'

'You had—you did?' she questioned, her eyes widening. She remembered that Saturday. 'I'd gone for a walk—and started out for your grandmother's around lunchtime. Um—you—wanted to get in touch to ask why

I needed her phone number?' she queried, her brain racing but few answers arriving.

'That,' Yorke confirmed, 'and to tell you how Rod had written confessing everything, with your friend's written endorsement that it was her wish that you return the ring to me.'

'But—when you couldn't reach me—when I wasn't in—you decided not to tell me about your cousin's letter after all?' she pressed, none of it making sense. Yorke had wanted that ring. All he'd had to do was to show her that letter and it would have been his.

'When you weren't in I felt—strangely for me—totally at a loose end.' Strangely? Sabina supposed it would be strange for him. She had an idea that Yorke would be busy enough at work or play to be able to fill every waking hour. 'On the spur of the moment, instead of ringing my grandmother to enquire how she was, I decided to drive down to see for myself how she was.'

'Ah!' Sabina exclaimed. 'You found me there and were furious that I'd taken it upon myself to seek her out.'

'I'd no idea what upsetting shocks you had given or might be planning to give her.'

'Thanks!' Sabina muttered tightly.

'Forgive me, my dear,' Yorke apologised at once, his 'my dear' shaking Sabina far more than that the great Yorke Mackinnon should apologise for anything. 'In the anger of the moment, I forgot entirely all about the splendid sensitivity I'd seen in you.' Oh, don't, Sabina wanted to beg, her heart racing. 'It *was* some time since I'd actually seen you,' he defended.

Yorke? Defending? Just the fact that that was what he seemed to be doing sent her defences flying. But— she had to be strong. Attacking. 'Even when you knew I was there at your grandmother's invitation, you were still furious,' she charged.

'But you showed me what I could do with my fury by—to my amazement, I own—taking me on when I goaded you into accepting my grandmother's invitation to stay overnight. You, Sabina Constable,' he added, without knowing it sending her brain patterns haywire, 'are one hell of a woman.'

He thought that? She, of cautious, don't-ripple-the-water fame? 'Few women would sit still for that!' she tossed at him as airily as she was able. 'And that still doesn't explain why it's taken all this time for you to tell me about this letter.' Having forgotten that she still held Rod's letter in her hand, she waved it at Yorke.

'I intended to—several times. Believe me,' he stated. 'But—' He broke off. Hesitated. And, even though she could not believe what her eyes were telling her, he suddenly seemed—and she knew it was crazy—strangely unsure of himself.

'But?' she prompted, discounting the evidence of her senses. Yorke? Unsure? Pfff!

He looked at her, those dark eyes boring into her suddenly. As if—as if first, before he went on, he needed something from her. Some kind of—assurance from her. It definitely was crazy, she decided. Yorke was the most assured man she had ever known.

'But,' he took up, without her assurances, deciding to go on and, as if he could do no other, take the risk, 'since knowing you my intentions and acting on those intentions have been greatly at variance with each other.'

'You're blaming me for that?'

'Hell, no,' he at once denied. 'Although...' Again he hesitated—and then sent her world spinning when, his tone even, he confessed, his eyes steady on hers, 'You've been getting to me in a big way, Sabina.'

Her mouth went dry, her heart started to pound. She needed help. What was he saying? What *was* he saying?

'I—um...' She swallowed. She tried for a scornful note—it didn't quite come off. 'Since when?' she asked.

In fact it didn't come off at all—for Yorke saw her question not as sarcasm but as an invitation, and hesitated no longer. 'Since the first moment I saw you, was in company with you, experienced at first hand the spirit in you, the loyalty in you, since then I knew—that there was something different about you.'

This was getting miles away from the question of why he had waited this long to tell her about his cousin's letter. But Sabina just then had no thought to remind him. 'You—er—saw all that in our first meeting?' she just had to query, striving hard to keep a sane head.

Yorke nodded. 'And more. At our second meeting, when I came here to collect my grandmother's ring—and told you she was in hospital—I immediately saw what a very soft heart you have. I confess, my dear, that I played on your soft heart, took advantage to press home why it was so important that I returned that ring to her.'

'But I wouldn't let you have it,' Sabina commented, Yorke's confessing to playing on her heartstrings in the cause of his grandmother's health as nothing as her heartbeats again raced at his 'my dear'—even if it meant nothing. What the dickens would it mean? Oh, grief!

'You would not, and I was ready to strangle you for your obstinacy—and then I had this idea...'

'That I should pretend to be engaged to you.'

'And you, not without argument, agreed.'

'I agreed just to go to the hospital—and for one visit only,' she reminded him.

But he had forgotten nothing, it seemed, and took up, 'I thought you'd decided against it, when eventually, forty-five minutes late, you arrived for that visit. As angry with you as I was, though, I thought for the look of it I'd better kiss your cheek.'

'You didn't, you kissed...' She halted. Oh, heavens, it would have been better if she'd said nothing.

'I kissed your lips, your lovely mouth.' Yorke seemed to see no reason not to finish for her. Indeed, he even appeared to have gained some encouragement that she had so remembered. Encouragement! What encouragement did he need? Was she going totally off her head? 'And,' he continued, his dark eyes holding hers, somehow refusing to let her look away, 'since I somehow didn't seem able to resist stealing that kiss, I then discovered I was most reluctant to break away.'

Her eyes went huge in her face. What was he *saying*? Oh, what could he mean? 'Well—you're an—er—a virile man,' was the best she could come up with.

He shook his head. 'Hardly. With my grandmother there?'

'Hardly,' she agreed. 'But you were still mad at me when we went out to the hospital car park.'

'Why wouldn't I be? I asked you to have dinner with me—and you had the nerve to tell me you had a dinner date with another man!'

'You said you'd buy me a sandwich!'

'I meant have dinner with me.'

Sabina stared at him, barely believing any of this conversation—though with no intention of putting a stop to it—not now. Not just yet—only if things got heated, or too much to handle. Whatever, Yorke must never guess at her feelings for him. Yet he sounded, marvellously, as if he objected to some other man taking her out to dinner!

'Our—er—"engagement"—was platonic.' She thought, in the interest of his continued good opinion, that she should remind him.

'Was it?' he questioned—and as she remembered— oh, my word, how could she ever forget?—being nearly naked in his arms, her cheeks went pink.

'It was meant to be,' she replied as primly as in the circumstances she could.

'But I kissed you, and wanted to go on kissing you,' he owned, and she wished he would kiss her then or at least hold her because the ground she was on had never felt shakier and she had never felt more vulnerable than she did at that time.

She no longer wanted him sitting there where he could see into her face. But, since she did not want him to go—not yet—not ever—she got up and went over to the window, to tweak an imaginary crease out of the curtain, to stare out. And to very nearly go into heart failure, when, not having heard him move, Yorke came to the back of her and, taking a hold of her arms, turned her to face him.

Sabina looked up into his dark, penetrating eyes and down again. She could read nothing in his look, but was so afraid of what he might see in hers. 'You're trembling,' he murmured softly somewhere above her head. He still held her arms. She tried to pull out of his hold but he would not let her. Then she was going nowhere in a hurry for he told her gently, 'I won't hurt you,' adding amazingly, softly, 'Don't you know, Sabina, that I care for you?'

Her trembling increased on the instant. Instinctively she wanted to look up to see what was in his face. But she hadn't been able to gauge anything from his expression before—and positively did not want him seeing in hers that the fact that he cared for her should mean so much.

So she stayed with her head bent. But a moment later had her wish of a minute or so ago to be held by him when he breathed, 'Oh, dear, dear Sabina,' and, taking that step closer, pulled her gently into the circle of his arms. He made no attempt to tilt her head up or to kiss her but seemed content for the moment to hold her close up against him, as if he too needed that contact of her head resting on his chest. 'You're not afraid of me?' he asked after a while. She shook her head. 'Of this—emotion—that's between us?'

The ground beneath grew suddenly shakier. To agree to this—emotion between them seemed *too* open. After all, Yorke had merely said that he cared for her. And while that could mean a little or— She did not dare think. What she knew was that she needed something much more definite than that.

Sabina took a shaky breath and, drawing on all of her courage, asked huskily, 'What is between us, Yorke?'

'Honesty,' he answered disappointingly. 'From now on, only honesty.'

'You're suggesting I've been dishonest?' she questioned, stiffening slightly in his hold.

'Not you—me,' he replied unhesitatingly. 'Your honesty shines from you and I knew I could believe you when, in that hospital car park, you said that as soon as your friend gave her consent you would return that ring to me. But I, Sabina, by withholding the contents of that letter, have been less than honest with you. My only defence...' he paused, before adding quietly, '...is that I've been less than honest with myself.'

She looked up then; she had to. His face, his expression, was unsmiling, sincere. 'Oh,' she said, her mind in a quagmire to know where all this was leading. She felt confused—and pulled out of his arms. She needed to clear her head and, when he let go of her, wanted to be back in his arms again. 'Um...' she mumbled, and was suddenly afraid that, without saying more, he would leave. 'Well—OK,' she agreed, and then, managing a halfway decent shrug, 'So I suppose I am—er—a little interested, after all.' His smile was beautiful to see—her legs felt shaky. 'Shall we go and sit...?' Her voice faded when, taking her by the arm, Yorke led her not back to the chair she had been seated in but to the couch. And her thoughts went all haywire again when, preferring the couch himself to his chair, he came and sat beside her. 'You said you'd been less than honest with yourself,' she picked out of a jumbled-up nowhere, his letter that she had once been holding somehow now residing on the coffee-table beside her letter.

Yorke half turned so he could see fully into her face. Then, to her astonishment, he confessed, 'Emotions, all new to me since I met you, have turned the sane world as I knew it upside down.' Had she said she was a 'little' interested? Ye gods, she was avid to know more.

'Emotions?' Her voice was a whisper of sound, her eyes huge in her face. Yorke took a hold of her hand.

'Jealousy,' he stated, and while her heart thundered furiously away he elucidated, 'I didn't recognise it for that emotion at first, but I have to tell you, my dear, that on the evening that we met I was not at all taken with the notion that you were engaged to my cousin.'

Sabina stared at him, transfixed—but recalled, though hardly knew how she did in the circumstances, 'You thought at that time that I was Natalie.'

'I'd never met her, but when I saw you—beautiful, spirited, your wonderful eyes flashing sparks—something began happening in me.'

'Oh?' she queried guardedly, wishing he would tell her more, and with all speed, but panic that he was planning to drop her from a great height at any moment now trying to gain a foothold. 'You covered it well,' she remarked, a shade coolly, she owned, as she remembered how she wasn't going to be humiliated, how she was going to be dignified.

Yorke quietly surveyed her ungiving expression, and after some moments said gently, 'Don't be afraid. I'll never harm you.'

Oh, Yorke! Her backbone all but melted. 'I'm—n-not sure what you're trying to say,' she stammered at last.

'Forgive me,' he apologised immediately. 'This is such new territory for me, and I confess I'm at such pains to know the outcome, that what with my anxieties and everything else I'm not surprised I'm getting it wrong.'

Good heavens—he was suffering anxieties too! 'You—er—said something about feeling—um—strangely for you—at a loose end.' She caught at a stray something he had said in a sudden need to help him out.

His thumb rubbed over the back of the hand he was holding, and while everything in her tingled he recalled, 'That was when, not having seen you for what seemed an age, you weren't in when I called—so I went down to my grandmother's place. I hadn't realised how much I'd missed you.'

'You missed me! But we'd only met a couple of times!' she exclaimed.

'Three,' he corrected. 'But I wasn't acknowledging then anything so concrete as the fact that while I'd felt restless the whole time I was in Japan I should feel plain out of sorts because you weren't home when I called. Nor could I deny the surge of adrenalin that spurted through me on seeing your car parked on my grandmother's drive—despite my immediate fury.'

'You were afraid I'd sought her out so I could tell her the truth about her ring—that Rod had stolen it?' Sabina suggested.

'I knew, as soon as I spotted the ring on your finger, that you'd said nothing.'

'But you were still mad.'

'Why wouldn't I be? I said I'd missed you for my grandmother's ears—and was amazed that as I said it I realised it was the truth.'

'Honestly?' she asked, still trying to take it in.

'Only honesty now,' he stated, and, while her bones melted, added, 'Why else, when what I should have been doing was seeing to it that you were away from my grandmother's place with all speed, should I, half in anger, half because of missing you, goad you into staying longer at Mulberry House?'

'You wanted me to stay overnight?' she gasped.

'I wasn't into admitting it then, but oh, yes, lovely Sabina,' he agreed softly, 'I wanted you near.'

'You're—serious?' she asked chokily, her insides all over the place at what she thought he was telling her.

'Never more so,' he confirmed.

'We—er—had a row. That day, when you came with me to my room, we had a row,' she reminded him out of the blue as she tried, helplessly, to keep her feet firmly on the ground.

'And I ended up kissing your warm, inviting mouth,' he remembered. 'I sensed then, when I wanted to kiss you again, and keep on kissing you, that I was losing it.'

'Is that why you left my room so quickly?' she asked, amazed.

He nodded, and smiled, and told her ruefully, 'I'd fully intended to tell you all about Rod's letter. But we started to fight—and then we kissed—I knew I had to get out.'

'Good heavens!'

'And, for my sins, I found I couldn't get the sweetness of your lips from my mind.'

'I didn't think you'd given that kiss another thought,' she shyly confessed.

'Oh, love,' he murmured, touching a finger to the side of her face. 'And there were you the next time I saw you talking of telling my parents the truth—and while I knew I should be agreeing there was something in me that just didn't want it over—not yet.'

'Not yet'—did he mean he wanted it over now? Sabina had never felt more mixed up in her life. But Yorke, as if he sensed a little of her confusion, raised her hand to his lips and gently kissed the back of it.

'You did that—at dinner—that night,' she reminded him jerkily.

'I couldn't help it. I should have known then that it was all up with me,' he smiled, but went on, 'I knew you were troubled by your conscience. But, as I looked at you so my heart started to pound, and I acknowledged—for the first time—that there was something very special about you, Sabina Constable.'

His heart had started to pound! Her heart was positively blasting away to know that she'd had that sort of effect on him. 'My—hmm—you—' She stopped, and tried again. 'I felt enormously pulled to state the truth,' she found out of thin air in her need for something to steady her. 'But when I looked at Mrs Fairfax she looked so frail and—'

'I have to tell you, tender-hearted that you are,' Yorke interrupted, 'that prior to her illness my grandmother, while having the constitution of an ox, always appeared delicately frail. But you were so sensitive that night, and my emotions once my parents had driven off were in such a riot—I was too shaken to so much as bid you goodnight.'

'You felt that way too!' she exclaimed.

'You're saying that you were confused—afraid to touch, afraid to speak? Afraid—?' He broke off, stared at her, seemed to draw a great deal of strength from just looking at her, and just had to lean forward—and kiss

her. It was a gentle kiss, a lovely kiss, and when Yorke
pulled back to study her mesmerised face he just had to
lean forward and kiss her again. 'Oh, my dear,' he said,
and looked as though he might kiss her a third time.
But ruefully he shook his head, as though, for the
moment, there were more important matters to be resolved. 'And you spent most of that night worrying, and
stormed into my room at five insisting I tell my parents
the truth.'

'When all along you had a letter that...'

'I only meant to tease you a little,' Yorke confessed.
'It was in my mind to show you Rod's letter that morning
but—we kissed and it went clear out of my head.'

She hadn't been thinking at all herself then, Sabina
remembered, and marvelled that, by the sound of it, it
had been pretty much the same for him too. 'You've—
um—had time in between then and now to tell me,' she
overcame a moment of total weakness to mention.

'Plenty of time, plenty of opportunity,' he smiled.
'Thank God you don't hate me.' He waited, but when
he realised there was no way she was going to give him
an inkling of how she truly felt about him he gave
another rueful look and owned, 'There was a moment
when you knocked on my door for your robe when I
could have told you—only that got lost without trace
when you told me you were leaving, that you had a date
that afternoon, and I, so jealous I hardly knew what I
was saying, received a right upper-cut for my trouble.'

'Oh, Yorke,' she laughed, in the face of him admitting to jealousy his furious 'His bed or yours?' as
nothing. 'I'm sorry I hit you,' she apologised nicely.
'And,' she felt she also had to apologise, 'I'm sorry I
lied.'

'You lied?'

'I didn't have a date that afternoon,' she admitted.

Yorke looked at her solemnly, and then hinted, quietly, 'But you did have a date two evenings later.'

'I...' she was about to defend—and changed her mind. 'And so did you,' she pointed out as calmly as she was able.

'You wouldn't like to tell me that you were a tiny bit jealous, I suppose?' he fished. She shook her head. 'Tiny bit' was a misnomer but, although the ground she was on was starting to feel a touch firmer, she still, nervously, needed to keep guard—in case she was in for one enormous let-down. 'So why wouldn't I date someone?' he continued when Sabina refused to answer.

'Why wouldn't you?' she tossed back at him—a little prickly, she had to own.

And Yorke spotted her prickles and, as if he found some comfort at her small show of feeling that he should have dated some other woman, confessed, 'I was still feeling shattered from the effect making love with you had had on me, so Lord knows I didn't fancy other women.'

'From what I saw as I was leaving, you seemed totally engrossed in your dinner partner,' Sabina stated sniffily.

'You *were* jealous!' Yorke exclaimed, looking in no way unhappy about that. And when Sabina favoured him with an aloof look it was with a smile that he quietly questioned, 'Would it be of any help if I told you I spent too much time while you were in that restaurant secretly glancing to where you were, and that I was aware of your every move? That when you got up to go I watched you, and only looked from you when it looked as if you might turn round?'

'No!' she gasped.

'It's the truth,' he assured her.

'You—c-care for me—you said?' she just had to hint nervously.

And could hardly breathe when, his look gentle on her, he answered softly, 'My darling, I love you.'

A sharp breath took her, and she was so filled with wonder that she could not speak. 'You love me?' she choked when she was able.

'I love you. I adore you. And I'm going quietly demented trying to fathom if you care for me, if the hopeful signals I think I've seen have been just wishful thinking on my part. It's not just physical chemistry on your part, is it?' he questioned urgently. 'Say not. Say, my dear, dear love, that you love me.'

He sounded in torment! And Sabina could hold out no longer. 'Oh, I do,' she cried.

'You do—love me?'

'I do.'

'You're not just saying it to—?'

'I love you, I love you, I love you,' she assured him, near to tears in her joy—and knew nothing for the next five minutes when, with an exultant sound, Yorke gathered her into his arms.

He held her, pulled her close, pulled back so he could see into her face, and held her close again. Her heart was pounding, matching his for thunder, as she held him, kissed him when he kissed her, pulled back so she might see into his face, and loved him totally when he just had to kiss her again.

'When?' he asked at length, keeping a tight hold on her. 'Did it creep up on you as it did with me? Did it...?'

She shook her head, wallowing in his open look of adoration. 'Oh, Yorke,' she whispered. 'I was so busy hating you most of my time, I'd no idea I was falling in love with you— Well, I suppose there were indications along the way...'

'Tell me,' he insisted.

'Indications I was falling...?'

'Everything.'

'Including the way you make me feel weak at the knees when you grin in a certain fashion?'

Yorke looked at her, seemed hardly able to believe he had that effect on her. 'Including that,' he murmured, adding, 'Did you know you have a look that quite devastates me when you're dying to laugh but are determined not to?'

'No!' she gasped, having had no idea.

'True,' he stated, and, seeming anxious to have more confirmation of her love for him, he hinted, 'Indications?'

'Well . . .' she obliged. Yorke loved her! He loved her! 'Indications... When I'd quite liked the look of someone but—after meeting you—when he asked me out I discovered I wasn't too fussed about going.'

'I should think so,' he stated heavily, and she loved him and loved him and laughed—and he just had to kiss her. 'So?' he questioned after some long moments of just feasting his eyes on her.

'So,' she replied while she tried to get her mind back on what they had been talking about. Yorke was, it seemed, insisting on knowing everything about her love for him. 'So, it was that Sunday morning down at your grandmother's. We were on your bed and so close and I just knew an urge to tell you that I loved you.'

'You knew then?'

'I did,' she owned. 'You asked me, "What do you know?" and I just knew it. I loved you. I hoped, of course, that it was just the—er—heat of the moment.'

'But it wasn't?' He looked anxious. Unbelievably, her heart playing ducks and drakes with her, Yorke actually looked anxious lest her love for him be a thing of the moment.

She shook her head. 'No. It was still there the next time I saw you. Even while I was annoyed with you, furious with you—I still loved you.' She smiled, adored

his look of love, the gentle yet thrilling kiss he bestowed
on her, and, when she was somewhere near sensible, she
just had to ask, 'And you, Yorke; when...?' She did
not have to finish.

'Love for you crept up unannounced,' he revealed.
'Though first, while in my mule-headed way I refused
to recognise it, I had to go through a whole gamut of
other emotions.'

'Jealousy?' Sabina suggested cheerfully.

'How can you look so cheerful when I've been through
such torment?' he scolded, not looking too unhappy
about it now that he knew that she loved him. 'Jealousy
is a most unreasoning emotion,' he stated.

'I know,' Sabina said gently. She didn't want him to
hurt any more.

Nor, it appeared, did Yorke want her to hurt any more,
because he wasted no more time to tell her, 'My companion at that restaurant, by the way, was merely an
acquaintance, nothing more. I couldn't, or wouldn't,
understand why you were in my head so much, and why
I didn't feel like dating anybody.'

'So you dated her...'

'To try—without success—to get you out of my head.'

'You say the nicest things,' she smiled, and was kissed.

'Witch!' he becalled her lovingly. 'I knew full well,
of course, that night, that what I should be doing was
acquainting you with the contents of that letter. But there
you were, looking elegant, sophisticated—and uppity
with it. I was certain you were all set to ignore me.'

'Oh, dear. You weren't going to have that.'

'Minx! I was fuming— Who the hell does she think
she is? Jealous— How dare you date somebody else?'

'You'd forgotten your blonde date, of course.'

'Who's telling this?' he grinned.

'So you kissed me to put me in my place—and even
had the nerve to ask for that ring!' she remembered.

'Did I mention I was furious as well as jealous?' She kissed him. The kiss lengthened, and she felt quite dizzy when eventually Yorke allowed some daylight between their two bodies. She had only a vague memory of why she had kissed him, and Yorke was looking equally hazy, but, after a few more seconds, recovered. 'Is it any wonder that you haunted my dreams that night?' he asked. What could she do? She smiled her delight. 'The very next day I decided to come and see you,' he smiled back. 'Decided to get it all said and done—show you that letter, take the ring and then, with everything over—perhaps then you'd be out of my head.'

'You never said any—'

'I didn't get chance to say very much at all. There were you when I called—in next to nothing, clearly expecting some Oliver bod, and—'

'I was dressed perfectly respectably to listen to an old friend—who incidentally I've known since I was about three—bemoan or otherwise the current state of his love-life.'

'He's a friend from way back?' Yorke looked mightily relieved.

'We met at toddlers' group,' she laughed. 'I love him like a brother.'

'Thank God for that!'

Sabina loved the heartfelt sound of his remark and admitted, 'I wasn't expecting Oliver, actually—or anyone else,' she added quickly. And confessed for good measure, as she thought she ought, 'When the phone rang that night it was, as I thought, my mother. So I couldn't let you answer it.'

'She'd have wanted to know who I was?'

'Most definitely.'

'Shall we drive over and see her later—and your father, of course?' Yorke suggested, adding quickly, 'I know you said when I arrived you've things to do today that don't include me, but now that I know you love me I can't bear to let you out of my sight.'

'I lied. About having things to do,' she added quickly, lest he should think she meant about telling him that she loved him. He kissed her, and looked the happiest she had ever seen him as she offered, 'I'd love to spend my day with you.'

'More than that, I hope,' he replied, and her heart thundered at his hint that he wanted to spend more time with her than just today. 'But, to get back to that Wednesday evening, I never did get round to showing you my cousin's letter, because our chemistry took off again. Then you were asking me to leave and, with my control near to breaking, I thought I better had—without delay.'

'Oh, if only I'd known.'

Gently, he kissed her, as aware as she of the harsh words they'd exchanged. 'If it's any consolation, my sweet darling, I've been slowly going off my head ever since then. Wanting to come and see you, knowing the futility of that. And what did I care anyway? So why was I detouring, sometimes many miles out of my way, purely to come by here?'

'You...!' Sabina was shaken. 'Honestly?' she questioned, her mouth agape.

'Ridiculous, isn't it?'

'Wonderful,' she answered softly, still finding it incredible. 'You didn't think to come in?'

'Once. But that damned Morgan was parked behind your car again, so unless someone was thoughtlessly in the habit of parking behind you and blocking you in I knew you had a visitor. It was come up and bust him on the jaw or go home.'

'Oh, Yorke!' He'd been that jealous!

'Who owns it, Oliver or Christopher?' he wanted to know.

'Oliver. Chris is the man I was having dinner with. The one I thought I wanted to go out with but...' It seemed disloyal, and Chris had always been very pleasant. 'He's nice,' she said.

'I'll take your word for it.'

'I can see you're impressed,' she teased, and when he had to smile she sighed, 'Oh, I do love you.'

'As I love you, my dear love,' Yorke breathed. And, holding her tightly to him, he said, 'It's been hell, sweetheart, giving in to this love that had me licked before I'd got started.'

'When did you give in?' Sabina asked, still wanting to pinch herself that this really was happening. 'When did you know—that you loved me?'

'Last night!' he answered without hesitation. Though he qualified, 'Or rather in the early hours of this morning.' Sabina sat rapt, hanging on his every word. 'I'd been out to a business dinner, as I told you,' Yorke continued. 'But, since I seemed to have done a lot of restless pacing about my apartment just lately, I suddenly found it too constricting, and took myself off for a walk.'

'At that time of night?'

'When you can't sleep, love, you can't sleep.' Didn't she know it? 'And sleep seemed light years away. So I walked—with you in my head for company. But when I get back, there—can I believe my eyes?—are you.'

'I couldn't sleep either,' she openly confessed, and was pulled closer to him.

'You're beautiful,' he breathed softly, and she adored him, and he went on to tell her of his thoughts and feelings when he'd come back from his walk not that many hours ago and seen her outside where he lived. 'At first I feared that something was wrong,' he began, and at once Sabina remembered how she had thought—

and immediately discounted it—that he had sounded as though he cared that something might be wrong.

'I intended merely to pop a letter in, only...'

'Only I arrived home and, I confess, it was so wonderful to see you after all that while that nothing would do but that I seize the chance to spend some time with you.'

'Really?'

'Believe me, sweet love. Even while my thoughts were shooting off in all directions, wondering what had brought you to my door, a conviction was growing in me that I did not want to tell you of Rod Lacey's letter, that I did not want to end what through him—the only reason that we knew each other—had begun. But, before I knew it, that old green-eyed monster was having a go at me again, and once more—to let me know, in case I didn't, that nobody speaks to you like that and gets away with it—we were fighting again.'

'And—kissing,' Sabina inserted dreamily.

'And kissing,' Yorke agreed softly. 'And there it was! Suddenly, just like that, I knew that I loved you to distraction. That I was in love with you with the whole of my being.'

'Oh, Yorke,' she sighed blissfully. She had known 'just like that' too.

Gently he kissed her, held her close for an empathetic moment or two, before revealing, 'My love for you was there before then, but that was when it landed. And all I knew then was that I wanted to be with you always.' Oh, how marvellous that sounded! Her insides went like jelly. 'And to never let you go. I wanted to protect you, to tell you how I felt—but we were making love, and then, out of this love I have for you, this need I have to protect you, I just then knew I would hate it if you thought I was telling you I loved you as just—and only— part and parcel of my having my way with you.'

'Oh, darling,' she whispered shyly—and was rewarded by such a look of love that her heart turned over.

Then Yorke was confessing, 'It was then that everything in my head went shambolic— Hey, what was I thinking about—was I presupposing that you loved me? You weren't hanging back in our lovemaking, but that didn't mean for a moment that you returned my love... Little Sabina, there was I, ready to tell you of my love, and there were you, so trusting—somehow I had to find the strength to deliberately step back from you.'

'Was that the reason?' she gasped. 'I thought it was because I was too—er—eager—responsive.' Yorke looked a shade stunned that she could think that, and she felt her cheeks go a tinge pink.

'Oh, little love,' he breathed. 'You're wonderful. And, whether you know it or not, there was such an innocence in your response, a shyness too, for all you felt you were over-responsive, that I, in my love for you, had to guard. I was afraid to so much as kiss you again.'

'Truly?' she gasped, her eyes growing huge in her face.

'Believe me, my dear one,' he smiled gently. 'It was about then that I suddenly started to feel more vulnerable in that situation than I felt you were. And all I knew was that I needed to sort my head out before I took you in my arms again. Then I was flattened by the immediate thought that, oh, hell, before I did anything I had to be honest and open with you and tell you about the ring—Rod's letter. And a nightmare started inside me.'

'Oh, Yorke,' she sympathised softly. 'But you couldn't tell me then?'

'Not then. I was vulnerable, as I said—not thinking straight. You were in a state and I was in a state—and while all hell was breaking loose in me there was weather outside to match.'

'And you wouldn't let me go home,' she smiled, realising only then that, along with his concerned 'What's wrong?' when he'd come across her outside his home, his refusing to allow her to drive back to hers had all been part of his caring for her.

'I would not,' he agreed, 'and left you, afraid to lay so much as a finger on you, and nowhere near as in control as I was trying to show. And, in consequence, spent a wakeful night wrestling with, Did you care for me, and why should you? Torn in two questioning, Did you respond to me from pure chemistry? You were not promiscuous—I knew that for a fact—so were you perhaps a little in love with me? I'd been incensed at your easy references to Oliver—and Chris with his arm around you—I'd never known such violent, unreasoning emotion—so had it been a hint of that same jealousy I'd recognised when you'd asked if I had given up my women? I was certain by then that I was fooling myself—and yet I just didn't know how I'd be able to take it if, as I deserved, dear, loyal, darling that you are, you told me to get lost.' Sabina gave him a heartfelt look to show that there was not the remotest chance of that, not now, and he held her tightly, going on, 'I was up early, but had no idea that you'd gone until, with the time going on for eight, I couldn't stand the waiting any longer—and went to your room.'

'I'm sorry,' she apologised lovingly.

'So you should be,' he growled. 'There am I, shaken rigid that you've left without my knowing it, and still trying to get my head together from it—when I find you'd left the ring behind.'

'I'm glad you decided to come over,' she smiled, a hint of impishness in her look.

'Even though, heartless woman, your parting "don't ever come near me again" added to my nightmare?'

Sabina adored him. 'Sorry,' she apologised again—
and felt her heart start to flutter when Yorke said nothing
for a while, but stared at her for long, long moments.

She began to feel unaccountably nervous—she had
never seen him so serious. 'You know,' he began at last,
his eyes never leaving her face, 'you really will have to
break this newly acquired habit of yours of creeping off
home at the crack of dawn.' She stared back at him,
sensing that there was more to come than his reference
to her leaving Mulberry House so early that Sunday
morning—and leaving his home this morning when he'd
thought her still abed. 'I think, Sabina, my love, if it's
all right with you, that you'd better move in with me.'

'Move in with you?' she echoed, her eyes going wide
again as excitement, nerves and a little confusion too
jostled for front position.

'Please, if you would,' he confirmed, and, still in a
quiet, steady tone, while taking her left hand in his, said,
'I first met you, lovely Sabina, when I came looking for
my grandmother's ring. But I know now what my subconscious must have been telling me when I didn't tell
you about Rod's letter—that I do not want it back.'

'You—don't want it back!'

'I want you to have it,' he explained, and, while her
heart started to race again, he pushed a hand inside his
trouser pocket and, taking out the ring, slipped it on her
engagement finger.

'Yorke!' she gasped.

'If you don't like it, we'll choose something else, but...'

'You w-want us to be engaged?'

'Have you forgotten my grandmother said for me to
give this ring to the woman I want to marry?' he questioned gently.

'You—want me to marry you?'

'Why else do you think I want to see your
parents today?'

Oh, heavens, was Yorke saying that he wanted to ask her father's permission to marry her? 'But...' She was not truly protesting, just trying to cope with shock.

Though Yorke read it differently. 'Oh, my God!' he exclaimed hoarsely, and actually seemed to have lost some of his colour. 'I got it wrong! You don't want to marry me!'

'I do, I do,' Sabina rushed in, unable to bear his stricken expression.

His colour started to return. 'Never, ever give me a fright like that again,' he admonished. But he was all loving again when he suggested, and meant it, 'As a forfeit, I insist that you marry me next week.'

'Next week!' she murmured faintly. But, as the thought took root, she sighed, 'Oh, how wonderful.' Then she said, knowing her mother would want her to have at least half a dozen bridesmaids and most definitely all the trimmings, 'My mother will kill you.'

Yorke didn't look in the least put off. 'What, me—the future father of her grandchildren?' he grinned, and with love in his eyes for his soon-to-be-bride—he kissed her.

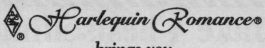

brings you

SIMPLY THE BEST

*Authors you'll treasure,
books you'll want to keep!*

Harlequin Romance just keeps getting better and
better...and we're delighted to welcome you to our
Simply the Best showcase for 1997, highlighting a
special author each month!

These are stories we know you'll love reading—again
and again! Because they are, quite simply, the best...

Don't miss these unforgettable romances coming to you
in May, June and July.

**May—GEORGIA AND THE TYCOON (#3455)
by Margaret Way
June—WITH HIS RING (#3459)
by Jessica Steele
July—BREAKFAST IN BED (#3465)
by Ruth Jean Dale**

Available wherever Harlequin books are sold.

Take 4 bestselling love stories FREE

Plus get a FREE surprise gift!

Special Limited-time Offer

Mail to Harlequin Reader Service®

3010 Walden Avenue
P.O. Box 1867
Buffalo, N.Y. 14240-1867

YES! Please send me 4 free Harlequin Romance® novels and my free surprise gift. Then send me 6 brand-new novels every month, which I will receive months before they appear in bookstores. Bill me at the low price of $2.67 each plus 25¢ delivery and applicable sales tax if any*. That's the complete price and a savings of over 10% off the cover prices—quite a bargain! I understand that accepting the books and gift places me under no obligation ever to buy any books. I can always return a shipment and cancel at any time. Even if I never buy another book from Harlequin, the 4 free books and the surprise gift are mine to keep forever.

116 BPA A3UK

Name	(PLEASE PRINT)	
Address	Apt. No.	
City	State	Zip

This offer is limited to one order per household and not valid to present Harlequin Romance® subscribers. *Terms and prices are subject to change without notice. Sales tax applicable in N.Y.

UROM-696   ©1990 Harlequin Enterprises Limited

Free Gift Offer

With a Free Gift proof-of-purchase
from any Harlequin® book, you can receive
a beautiful cubic zirconia pendant.

This stunning marquise-shaped stone is a genuine cubic
zirconia—accented by an 18" gold tone necklace.
(Approximate retail value $19.95)

Send for yours today...
compliments of HARLEQUIN®

To receive your free gift, a cubic zirconia pendant, send us one original proof-of-purchase, photocopies not accepted, from the back of any Harlequin Romance®, Harlequin Presents®, Harlequin Temptation®, Harlequin Superromance®, Harlequin Intrigue®, Harlequin American Romance®, or Harlequin Historicals® title available at your favorite retail outlet, together with the Free Gift Certificate, plus a check or money order for $1.65 U.S./$2.15 CAN. (do not send cash) to cover postage and handling, payable to Harlequin Free Gift Offer. We will send you the specified gift. Allow 6 to 8 weeks for delivery. Offer good until December 31, 1997, or while quantities last. Offer valid in the U.S. and Canada only.

Free Gift Certificate

Name: _____

Address: _____

City: _____ State/Province: _____ Zip/Postal Code: _____

Mail this certificate, one proof-of-purchase and a check or money order for postage and handling to: HARLEQUIN FREE GIFT OFFER 1997. In the U.S.: 3010 Walden Avenue, P.O. Box 9071, Buffalo NY 14269-9057. In Canada: P.O. Box 604, Fort Erie, Ontario L2Z 5X3.

FREE GIFT OFFER 084-KEZ

ONE PROOF-OF-PURCHASE
To collect your fabulous FREE GIFT, a cubic zirconia pendant, you must include this original proof-of-purchase for each gift with the properly completed Free Gift Certificate.

084-KEZR

HARLEQUIN ROMANCE'S 40TH ANNIVERSARY SWEEPSTAKES
OFFICIAL RULES—NO PURCHASE NECESSARY

To enter, complete an Official Entry Form or 3" x 5" card by hand printing the words "Harlequin Romance's 40th Anniversary Sweepstakes," your name and address thereon and mailing it to: In the U.S., Harlequin Romance's 40th Anniversary Sweepstakes, P.O. Box 9076, Buffalo, NY 14269-9076, or in Canada to Harlequin Romance's 40th Anniversary Sweepstakes, P.O. Box 637, Fort Erie, Ontario L2A 5X3. Limit: one entry per envelope, one prize to an individual, family or organization. Entries must be sent via first-class mail and be received no later than 7/31/97. No liability is assumed for lost, late or misdirected mail.

Prizes: 150 autographed hardbound books (value $9.95 each U.S./$11.98 each CAN.). Winners will be selected in a random drawing (to be conducted no later than 8/29/97) from among all eligible entries received by D. L. Blair, Inc., an independent judging organization whose decisions are final.

IF YOU HAVE INCLUDED THREE HARLEQUIN PROOFS OF PURCHASE PLUS APPROPRIATE SHIPPING AND HANDLING ($1.99 U.S. OR $2.99 CAN.) WITH YOUR ENTRY, YOU WILL RECEIVE A NONAUTOGRAPHED 40TH ANNIVERSARY COLLECTOR'S EDITION BOOK.

Sweepstakes offer is open only to residents of the U.S. (except Puerto Rico) and Canada who are 18 years of age or older, except employees and immediate family members of Harelquin Enterprises, Ltd., their affiliates, subsidiaries, and all other agencies, entities and persons connected with the use, marketing or conduct of this sweepstakes. All federal, state, provincial, municipal and local laws apply. Offer void wherever prohibited by law. Taxes and/or duties on prizes are the sole responsibility of the winners. Any litigation within the province of Quebec respecting the conduct and awarding of a prize in this sweepstakes may be submitted to the Régie des alcools, des courses et des jeux. All prizes will be awarded; winners will be notified by mail. No substitution for prizes is permitted. Odds of winning are dependent upon the number of eligible entries received.

Any prize or prize notification returned as undeliverable may result in the awarding of that prize to an alternative winner. By acceptance of their prize, winners consent to use of their names, photographs or likenesses for purposes of advertising, trade and promotion on behalf of Harlequin Enterprises, Ltd., without further compensation unless prohibited by law. In order to win a prize, residents of Canada will be required to correctly answer a time-limited, arithmetical skill-testing question administered by mail.

For a list of winners (available after September 30, 1997) send a separate stamped, self-addressed envelope to: Harlequin Romance's 40th Anniversary Sweepstakes Winners, P.O. Box 4200, Blair, NE 68009-4200, U.S.A.

HR40RULES

Happy Birthday to

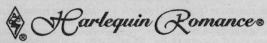

With the purchase of three Harlequin Romance books, you can send in for a **FREE** hardbound collector's edition and automatically enter Harlequin Romance's 40th Anniversary Sweepstakes.

FREE COLLECTOR'S EDITION BOOK

On the official entry form/proof-of-purchase coupon below, fill in your name, address and zip or postal code, and send it, plus $1.99 U.S./$2.99 CAN. for postage and handling (check or money order—please do not send cash), payable to Harlequin Books, to: In the U.S.: 3010 Walden Avenue, P.O. Box 9071, Buffalo, N.Y. 14269-9071; In Canada: P.O. Box 622, Fort Erie, Ontario L2A 5X3. Please allow 4-6 weeks for delivery. Order your **FREE** Collector's Edition now; quantities are limited. Offer for the free hardbound book expires December 31,1997. Entries for the Specially Autographed 40th Anniversary Collector's Edition draw will be accepted only until July 31, 1997.

WIN A SPECIALLY AUTOGRAPHED COLLECTOR'S EDITION BOOK

To enter Harlequin Romance's 40th Anniversary Sweepstakes only, hand print on a 3" x 5" card the words "Harlequin Romance's 40th Anniversary Sweepstakes," your name and address and mail to: "40th Anniversary Harlequin Romance Sweepstakes"—in the U.S., 3010 Walden Avenue, P.O. Box 9076, Buffalo, N.Y. 14269-9076; in Canada, P.O. Box 637, Fort Erie, Ontario L2A 5X3. No purchase or obligation necessary to enter. Limit: one entry per envelope. Entries must be sent via first-class mail and be received no later than July 31, 1997. See back-page ad for complete sweepstakes rules.

Happy Birthday, Harlequin Romance!

Official Entry Form/Proof of Purchase

"Please send me my FREE 40th Anniversary Collector's Edition book and enter me in Harlequin Romance's 40th Anniversary Sweepstakes."

Name: _____

Address: _____

City: _____

State/Prov.: _____ Zip/Postal Code: _____

089-KEP

089-KEP